THE
PHANTOM
OF
WALKAWAY HILL

OTHER YEARLING BOOKS YOU WILL ENJOY:

THE PHANTOM OF WALKAWAY HILL

Edward Fenton

A YEARLING BOOK

Published by
Dell Publishing
a division of
Bantam Doubleday Dell Publishing Group, Inc.
666 Fifth Avenue
New York, New York 10103

ISBN: 0-440-40476-2

Reprinted by arrangement with the author

Printed in the United States of America

July 1991

10 9 8 7 6 5 4 3 2 1

OPM

FOR KATE OF HICKS HILL,
who hates being left out of anything,
with apologies.

CONTENTS

THE
PHANTOM
OF
WALKAWAY HILL

1

I

Before I start, I think you ought to know that this is going to be a dog story as much as anything. It is really a shaggy-dog story. What I mean is, it's the story of a shaggy dog.

A few days before all the things in this story happened, I received a letter from Obie and Amanda. They wrote it together, although Amanda wrote most of it, especially all the parts with exclamation marks.

Dear James: [it said]

Well, we're in like Flynn. And we think we are going to like it here! Actually, the place is sort of overwhelming! As you will see.

How soon can you come? Because we need your help.

Something ominous is afoot! We cannot explain just

what in a letter. However, there are unseen presences about, and although we haven't yet found out what it is, we suspect something is going on! Of course *they* are so infatuated with the whole idea and the plans and moving things around and getting the house ready that they don't seem to have noticed anything strange. But then grown-ups never do seem to notice much anyway.

So please come up as soon as you possibly can and help us track it down because we are convinced there is a true mystery here somewhere.

We will tell you more when we see you.

Amanda and Obie.

P.S. The mystery part is still a secret. Amanda.
P.P.S. I think Amanda is exaggerating a little. Obie.
P.P.P.S. I am not! It really is very ominous as you will see when you get here. Amanda.

Well, there it was, and naturally I was wild to go and see what was up, even though I agreed with Obie about Amanda. She always does exaggerate a little. What I didn't know then was how really right she was this time.

And that's how this book came to be written.

I have always hated any book that started out with "I." I mean the kind of story that the hero tells himself, where he's very modest and apologetic, but all the time he's really telling you what a great guy he is and how he does all sorts of terrific things just in the nick of time, with his right hand practically tied behind his back.

Well, this isn't going to be that kind of story. But I'm afraid the only way it can get told is by me. At least I'm not the hero, which is something, so I don't have to pretend to be modest. I think that kind of pretending is stupid, anyway. My point is that if someone really does something terrific he might just as well admit it and get all the credit he can. Still, that's only what I think. I've never had the chance to prove it.

Anyway, the Old Man—that's what my father calls himself, although he doesn't like it quite so much when *I* call him that—says I ought to write it all down and see how it comes out. He says pencils and paper are cheap enough and I can afford them out of my allowance, which I might add is a far from princely sum, especially when you're trying to put a little something by for something you might want later on when you are old enough to have a driver's license. So you can see that this is going to be a sacrifice for me in more ways than one.

Personally, I think Amanda or Obie ought to write it, since it all really happened more to them than it did to me. I was just there at the time. But Amanda claims that she can't spell, which I told her straight out is pretty silly for her to maintain, since she's always writing those secret poems of hers. Well, she just got a lofty look on her face and answered that in poetry it's the thought and not the spelling that counts, which only proves that you can always trust a girl to back out of the picture when it comes to a showdown. And although Obie can take any pile of hopeless old junk and make something terrific out of it, he never could string three words together on paper and make sense. Obie, for reasons which you will understand in a minute, is Uncle Oliver's despair. Uncle Oliver being Obie and Amanda's father.

So I guess it really is up to me after all. I mean, somebody had to write this story and I seem to be stuck with the job. And the Old Man says that I have "the spectator's objective eye," which sounds good, but I'm not sure that it means too much.

Before I get any deeper, I think you ought to know

right off that I've never written anything before. I don't mean compositions about "The Most Exciting Holiday I Ever Spent" and all that sort of guff. They don't count. What I mean is a real book. And I don't mind admitting that I feel sort of funny beginning this. The whole idea gives me a watery feeling around the belt, as though I had a considerable aquarium there and didn't know what to do with it.

I talked to Uncle Oliver about it the other day. I figured he ought to be able to pass on a few valuable pointers about getting started, since he's a writer. In fact, he's the celebrated Oliver Little. You've probably read lots by Little. His books are all over the place. There's *Hal Sterling: Eagle Scout; Hal Sterling: College Freshman; Hal Sterling: Cub Reporter*, and so on, right down the line. In my opinion, Hal Sterling is too much of a hero. For one thing, he's so darned noble. Personally, I wish Uncle Oliver would kill him off, or something equally drastic, like getting him married, and put an end to him. I'd never say this to Uncle Oliver's face. It might make him discouraged, as I suppose he's pretty attached to Hal Sterling by now. And anytime the Littles have anything new they always say it's a present from Hal Sterling. Aunt Claire says all her tableware is Hal Sterling silver. But enough of that.

Anyway, when I broached the subject of my writing this story, Uncle Oliver looked at me kind of queerly. He straightened up a lot of blank paper on his desk. Then he said, "Look here, James. I've been thinking of doing something with it myself, except that right now I have to get Hal Sterling back from Outer Space."

I said I didn't mind a bit if he wanted to write the story instead of me. I meant it, too. Hope springs eternal.

He said: "But I'm not sure when I'll be able to tackle it.

I promised my publishers that when Hal returns from Outer Space, he'll go on a Special Mission to Moscow." Then he said, "No, I suppose somebody else in the family ought to begin carrying the torch."

He was probably referring to poor Obie, whose marks in English have always been terrible. Uncle Oliver has that way of talking sometimes, with his mouth twisted over to one side, so that you can't be sure if he means what he's saying, or is being sarcastic, or what. And so there I was, left holding the bag, so to speak.

"James," he said to me then, "I'd like to give you just one word of advice."

So I sat down. Whenever Uncle Oliver says "just one word," he generally means a couple of thousand. It all goes back to the days when he was still a struggling scribe and got paid according to the number of words that got printed. At least, that's what the Old Man says.

Anyway, I listened.

"And I want you to remember this," he said after a while. I figured he was winding up because his voice got very quiet, and from the owly way his eyes blinked behind his glasses I could tell that he really was going to tell me something important. "There are certain things, James, which no member of the writing profession should abide."

"Yes, Uncle Oliver?" I said.

"There are four of them: an untidy thought, a crabbed sentence, a confusing paragraph, a botched story."

Then he looked at me in a funny intent way, and that was it. The audience was over. So I thanked him and went away. I got my notebook and I wrote down those four things very carefully.

But I still didn't know how to start.

When I told the Old Man about it later, his face crinkled.

"Trust Oliver!" he said, but I don't think he meant it unkindly. Then he must have seen that I was still on the puzzled side, so he said, "James, if I were you, I'd start out by just saying the words. Let the story take care of itself. It'll come out somehow."

So that's what I'm doing now.

Now that all that is out of the way, I suppose I ought to introduce myself.

I'm James Gregory Smith, Junior. I wish people would call me Greg or Jim, but since the Old Man is Jim, I always end up being called James. Anybody who tries Junior or Smitty is practically begging for a dirty look.

I don't suppose you'd ever pick me out of a crowd, unless maybe my hair was combed, which it hardly ever is. I mean, life's too short for that kind of nonsense. I'm average size for my age, which is twelve, and right now I look practically ghoulish. That's because I have one tooth missing on the left side. I lost it last month when my school played Marlborough, which ought to show you what types Marlborough produces. The thing that really hurt wasn't the tooth but the fact that Marlborough won in spite of it. I go to the Bewick School, which isn't too bad, except for those lunches they give you: rice pudding practically every other day. My favorite sport is swimming and my hobby is collecting the "Criminals Wanted" posters that I fish out of the wastebaskets in the local post office. I have one hundred and three right now, and they really look great in my room. The best ones are right over my bed. The Old Man and I rattle around in a great big gloomy apartment that looks out over the park. The Old Man says that it didn't use to be so gloomy, and I guess he means when Mother was still alive. She died when I was small, so I can't really remember her, although sometimes I sort of think I can. I feel sorry for the Old Man sometimes. I mean, it must be lonely for him with only me, but he doesn't seem to want to do anything about it.

The Old Man and I get along pretty well together, except that I don't see too much of him. He's always taking off on some business trip or other. My best friends are my cousins Obie and Amanda Little, but they don't live in the city anymore, which is why this story happened in the first place. Amanda's birthday is on January 18, which makes her two days younger than I am, and Obie is a year older than we are. I'm not sure what I'm going to be when I finish going to school. If this book turns out any good, maybe I'll take up writing, but Uncle Oliver says it's a precarious vocation. Well, he ought to know.

And that takes care of Your Hero. Except that I'm not Your Hero or anybody else's. I'm just James. If there is anything more you want to know about me, it'll probably come out in the course of events.

All right.

It all happened last winter, during the longest, whitest weekend I ever spent anywhere. And it happened at Walkaway Hill.

2

WALKAWAY HILL

It was a perfectly ordinary Friday afternoon in March when the Old Man put me on the train. It was only a few days after I had received that letter from Obie and Amanda. I was pretty excited, but it wasn't only because of the letter. It was also because I was going to see their new home for the first time. I was too excited even to pay much attention to the wind that went whipping all over the place. Newspapers scudded along the sidewalks, and my coat flapped crazily around my legs, but there wasn't any hint of what was to come, which was probably a good thing. Otherwise, the Old Man might have made me stay home and then I'd have missed everything.

As it was, he was pretty generous. He bought me a stack of magazines and a pocketful of candy bars. "This ought to keep you busy until you get there," he said. And then he looked at me, sort of ruefully. "Give my love to all of them," he said. "Tell them I'll be up to inspect the place first chance I get. I wish I were going with you, but I couldn't tell those people from Washington not to come this evening."

Then he looked at his watch and scooted out to the platform. "Don't forget: Jonesboro is where you get off," he shouted through the window. "Uncle Oliver will meet you at the station."

"Okay," I called back with as much dignity as I could muster. After all, I could read my ticket, and I didn't want the people around me to think I was just a kid, traveling by himself for the first time. I mean, I'd been lots of places by myself before. Frankly, I was relieved when the train pulled out.

I settled back in my seat, opened a magazine, and got to work on the candy bars while I watched the scenery. Actually, I hate scenery, so I won't bother to describe any of it. Besides, I wasn't really paying much attention to what was on the other side of the window. I was too wound up. I knew every word in that letter by heart. If I'd known what was really in store, I don't think I'd have been able to sit there as calmly as I did. Of course, I should have had some inkling, because nothing that ever happens to the Littles is ordinary. Some people are like that. They can go out to post a letter and something terrific happens on the way, something really sensational in the adventure line. Other people can fly around the world and it'll be no more startling than reading the *National Geographic*. I suppose I ought to be used to the Littles by now, but as Uncle Oliver always says in his books, little did I realize, etc.

I guess I should have mentioned earlier that, ever since I can remember, Uncle Oliver and Aunt Claire had been talking about moving to the country. Uncle Oliver always said he was sure he could get started on that grown-up novel he'd always wanted to tackle if he didn't have the distractions of the metropolis all around him. He also said that with the world in such a turmoil it was a good idea to set one's roots down somewhere. And Aunt Claire was sure it would be much better for the children to live in the fresh air and have chores to do instead of mooning about in an apartment. And she had always wanted a garden of her own. She said, too, that the apartment was getting too small for all of them, what with all the books Uncle Oliver accumulated, and Obie's junk, and DeeDee getting too big to share Amanda's room. DeeDee is six, and although she is my own blood cousin, she is a spoiled brat and a pain in the side if ever I saw one. We all detest her. Well, anyway, Obie and Amanda and I do. The Old Man says she'll grow out of it in time, but we seriously doubt it.

The rest of the Little household consists of Mrs. MacMinnies, who came to help out when DeeDee was born and then just stayed on, and Sieglinde. Sieglinde belongs chiefly to DeeDee, which ought to be an indication. She is supposed to be a dachshund, but she looks more like an overstuffed frankfurter on legs. All she ever does is eat and sleep. I generally like dogs, but Sieglinde is something else again. Uncle Oliver says that for Sieglinde the world consists of four things—food, food, sleep, and food—which probably accounts for the fact that she can just manage to waddle from the kitchen to her basket and back again.

Well, there they all were, crammed into a medium-sized New York apartment, not far from ours, with Uncle Oliver griping about it daily and dreaming about his unborn novel, and Aunt Claire yearning for a garden, and Obie and Amanda wrangling over who was to take care of that pony they hoped to have. And then one day

Uncle Oliver announced that *Hal Sterling: Traveler in Time* was going to be made into a television series, which meant that they were now able to afford a down payment on a place in the country.

After that, Uncle Oliver and Aunt Claire drove out every single weekend to see real estate agents. I overheard them telling the Old Man what they wanted. The house had to be old, preferably genuine Colonial, with enough bedrooms for the whole family and overnight guests, a room where Uncle Oliver could write without distractions, and sufficient land for Aunt Claire to have her garden and Sieglinde not to get run over. "We want to be within two hours of New York," Uncle Oliver added, "so that I can go in to see my publishers whenever I have to, but it has to be isolated. I don't want to have to look at anybody else's television aerial." There was a great deal more about apple orchards and suitable schools in the neighborhood and stuff like that. But that was the gist of it.

The Old Man said, "It sounds like a tall order for what you're prepared to pay."

Uncle Oliver snorted, "Anyone who really knows what he wants is bound to find it eventually."

They looked and looked. Every Sunday they came back to the apartment more discouraged than ever. And then finally they called up to announce that they had found a terrific bargain. The place was practically being given away because the person to whom it belonged was in a nursing home and the lawyers wanted to sell it at once in order to avoid all the complications of waiting for probate and so on. They had to decide right away or they would lose it. Within a week they had bought it and moved in, and that was Walkaway Hill.

I don't mind admitting that things looked pretty bleak

for me with Obie and Amanda gone. Then Aunt Claire telephoned from the country, the day after the letter came, to say that they hadn't really settled in yet, but if we didn't mind sleeping among packing cases and cartons, we were welcome to come up for the weekend.

"I can't make it, Claire," I heard the Old Man say. "I've got these people coming from Washington on business."

I edged closer to the telephone. I didn't want to miss anything.

"What? Well, I suppose I could send James by himself since Obie and Amanda are so anxious to have him." There was a pause. Then he said, "Are you sure he won't be a nuisance to you right now?" and I was ready to disown him on the spot.

I heard Aunt Claire laughing. "Don't be silly, Jim," she said. "Send him along. We'll put him to work."

When the Old Man hung up he said to me, "Well, I guess it's all right for you to go up there Friday, after school." I dashed to my room and started packing. It was only Wednesday, but getting your stuff together for a weekend in the country is serious business. You never know what you're going to need.

So there I was on the train at last. I thought it would never get to Jonesboro. It stopped at every dinky station on the way. And all the time I was thinking about Walkaway Hill and what it would be like.

Naturally, I had a pretty clear idea. I knew it was going to be one of those ancestral places with white columns and weather vanes and low beams and winding stairs going mysteriously up and down all over the place. I'd read enough books, and I'd been to Mount Vernon once with the Old Man, so I knew the pitch. Even the name sounded wonderful: Walkaway Hill!

By the time the train got to Jonesboro I was pretty

keyed up. When I got out, I looked all over the station for Uncle Oliver. He wasn't anywhere in sight. For one terrible minute I thought I'd gotten off at the wrong stop, but it was Jonesboro, just as it said on my ticket.

I was standing there kind of dumbfounded when a tall rangy man came up to me. He had a thin bony face. An old felt hat all spattered with paint was jammed on his head and he had on a bright red lumber jacket.

He looked at me out of the saddest pair of brown eyes I'd ever seen. He grinned, but his eyes remained sad.

Then he said, "You're James, are you?"

I nodded.

"I'm Charlie Murofino. I'm supposed to collect you."

"Oh," I said.

"I'm doing a painting job over at the Houghton place, and I ran out of white, so I had to come into town anyway. No sense making two trips where one might do. That your bag? It looks kind of on the heavy side for a weekend."

"Well," I said, "you never can tell, can you?"

He nodded. "True enough," he said, and right away I decided that I liked him, even though I generally feel leery of thin people. I mean, I always feel most at ease with people who are on the fat and jolly side. But it didn't matter about Charlie Murofino's being so thin. I guess it was that grin of his that made the difference.

"There's your taxi," he said, pointing to a red pickup truck parked beside the station. It had his name painted on the side, and it was full of wonderful stuff: ladders and overalls and paint cans and tools and rusty old chains, all flung in every which way. He slung my suitcase on top of everything and we got in.

The truck started with a tremendous jolt and bounced through the town. Charlie waved at practically everybody. As soon as we passed a sign that said JONESBORO: TOWN LIMITS, it didn't even seem as though the wheels touched the road once. Charlie waved a hand at some mountains that loomed in the distance. "Those are the Berkshires over there," he told me, but the way we were bounding along didn't give me a chance to pay much attention to anything so unimportant as mountains.

"And that's where I live," Charlie said, waving his hand as we skimmed past a brightly painted ranch house with a picture window that looked right out on the road. There was a sign on the lawn: C. MUROFINO, PAINTER AND GENERAL CONTRACTOR. "Built it myself," he remarked matter-of-factly. I was impressed. "Everything looks kind of bleak right now," he said. He squinted at the sky. "Touch of snow in the air." Then he fell silent and we flew along a level stretch. "Have to watch out for those troopers," he shouted jauntily. "They nearly caught up with me last week." I didn't say anything. It was just as well, considering the way everything in the truck rattled.

We'd gone ten miles or so when Charlie turned to me. "That's quite a place Mr. Little's bought himself."

I didn't bother to answer. I figured I'd hear more that way.

"Yes indeed," Charlie Murofino went on. "It's been a regular white elephant. I know the place pretty well. I used to work for Mrs. Houghton, before I went into the navy. Mrs. Houghton is the woman that owned the place. Lived there all alone. She was a dilly. Fought with everybody. Nobody worked for her long. Eccentric, that's what she was. But then I guess she had enough money to be. She liked her own way. And she got it, generally. Trouble was that finally there wasn't anybody left for her to get it with."

"Oh," I said.

"And she died last week, a couple of days after your uncle bought the place. She'd been in a nursing home for a while before that. An artist, she was. Made statues. I don't know if they were any good. I liked some of them, though: the ones that weren't religious."

I sort of pricked up my ears at that. I mean, I've always been interested in art and all that stuff. I don't make a big thing about it, the way Amanda does, but I go over to the museum once in a while, and I think it's kind of exciting the way statues and paintings and things like that can stick around and stay alive for hundreds of years, long after the people who made them are gone. It sort of makes you stand still and think for a while.

"What happened to them?" I asked. I was wondering if they were in a museum, or something like that, where you could go and look at them.

Charlie just scratched his cheek.

"Funny thing," he said. "They disappeared. At least a lot of them did. Anyway, they weren't around when she died. And the Estate took away the ones that were left."

"The Estate?"

He nodded. "The lawyers and all who took care of everything after she died. Mrs. Houghton didn't have any relatives, not that anyone knew of, and she'd quarreled with everyone around here, so she didn't have any friends to leave her things to. So it's all in what they call the Estate." He grinned. "That's lawyers for you. They end up with everything."

The truck made a sharp turn. We shot up a narrow country road that I hadn't noticed. We followed it, bouncing and rattling, for quite a while. We passed hardly any houses. Then I saw a yellow mailbox among thick trees. Charlie stepped on the gas pedal and we swooped up a long lane. It was full of ruts and it seemed to go on forever, always climbing. Gravel splattered against the fenders: it sounded like a machine gun. Then, suddenly, the lane dipped and a barn flew by. We made a sharp turn after that. All of a sudden a house appeared, looming through a lot of tall dark evergreens. I smiled to myself, thinking of Uncle Oliver. It was isolated, all right. There wasn't anything in sight except for that barn and the woods and the hills all around.

And that was Walkaway Hill.

Only it wasn't at all what I had expected.

Right then, however, I didn't have time to take in much more than that because of the barking.

I'd never heard anything like it. It was wild and crazy and desperate and it went on and on, like the Hound of the Baskervilles or something. And what made it a lot weirder was that I couldn't be sure where it was coming from. I knew one thing: It wasn't Sieglinde.

Charlie shook his head.

"That must be Maggie," he said.

"Maggie?"

"Mrs. Houghton's old dog. She's still around the place."

"But I thought that Mrs. Houghton—"

"The lawyers paid somebody to stay on the property while she was sick. The only person they could get, though, was Barney Rudkin. He was the caretaker." Charlie sniffed. "Only there was more take than care to Barney, if you know what I mean." He shook his head again. "I never thought much of Barney. But he's gone now, and a good thing too."

"Gone?"

Charlie shrugged. "Yep. He went off somewheres right after the place was sold. Nobody's noticed him around since. Not that we'd of missed him," he added, grinning.

The barking was even wilder now and more desperate. Charlie frowned. "Maggie got sort of nervous after Mrs. Houghton was taken away," he said. "She's gotten even stranger ever since the day Mrs. Houghton died. You'd almost think she knew what had happened. Mrs. Houghton was the only one who could ever handle Maggie."

Just then something streaked across the front of the house. I couldn't be certain what it was. Then we heard the shouts. The next thing I knew Charlie had jammed on the brakes. The truck screeched to a violent halt. Charlie jumped out.

"Come on," he yelled. "Something funny is going on here."

3

THE SHAGGY DOG

Charlie Murofino dashed toward the house and I went after him.

The first impression I got was of a lot of confusion.

Then I stopped running and tried to make out what was happening.

There seemed to be a hundred people careering around, and the shouting was like Custer's Last Stand. Then I saw that actually it was only one stumpy little man holding a dog collar and a leash. He was all out of breath what with darting this way and that, and hollering. Obie was whooping like a Comanche and chasing in the other direction, while Uncle Oliver and Aunt Claire and Amanda and Mrs. MacMinnies and DeeDee all stood huddled in a clump by the front porch, staring. And then, to add to everything, Sieglinde, cowering like a fat lump of wurst at DeeDee's feet, started to yap.

There was too much going on for anyone to pay any attention to me.

Charlie called to the stumpy man, "What's up, Mr. Bodine?"

Mr. Bodine wiped his forehead with the back of his hand. "It's that blasted Maggie," he yelled hoarsely. "Give me a hand with her, will you, Charlie?"

Charlie grinned all the way from one ear to the other. "Why, you're not afraid of old Maggie, are you, Mr. Bodine?"

"This is no time for being funny, Charlie," Mr. Bodine answered, puffing. His face was all mottled. I wouldn't have been surprised to see him explode on the spot. "That lawyer in Jonesboro called me up and told me to fetch her. I'm supposed to board her in my kennels, but I can't lay my hands on her. I can't even get near her."

"No one ever could," said Charlie.

Then I saw the dog, racing toward the barn.

I don't think I'd ever seen a more bedraggled creature in my life before. She was a fair-sized collie, sort of the color of a lion, and she must have been a beauty to begin with, but her coat was all shaggy and matted with burrs. Twigs stuck out of her ruff where they were tangled in the long thick hair, and her white vest was caked gray with mud. Her tail dragged between her legs and there was a hunted look in her eyes. You couldn't help feeling sorry for her, she was so wild and neglected. And all the time she ran, she barked like a crazy thing.

"You go that way, toward the barn, Charlie, and head her off," Mr. Bodine hollered. "And you boys," he called to Obie and me, "you circle the other way. One of us ought to be able to grab her."

"Sure," said Charlie.

Well, we did our best, but that shaggy dog was more

than a match for us. No matter which way we went it was as though she knew what we meant to do before we did it. Once I thought Charlie had his hands on her mane, but she slipped through his fingers and was off again.

After about fifteen minutes of scrambling and stumbling after her we were ready to call it a day and give up. None of us had any breath left, and it was plain to see that Maggie was too canny to be caught. She kept at a safe distance, bounding in that stiff-legged way that collies have, making desperate wide circles around us and still barking. Whenever Mr. Bodine got within twenty yards of her she bared her teeth.

Uncle Oliver had been watching the whole performance with a kind of pained detachment written all over his face.

Mr. Bodine shrugged his shoulders. "It's no use," he said, and stuffed the collar and leash into his pocket. Then he went up to Uncle Oliver.

"Well, mister," Mr. Bodine said, "like I said before, I'm supposed to pick that dog up and take her down to my kennels until the Estate decides what's to be done about her. But I can't catch her. I don't think there's a man alive who can. Now the Estate don't want to leave her running loose this way. So there's only one thing left for me to do."

"Yes?" said Uncle Oliver.

"I'm going to have to shoot her. The place belongs to you now, so I just want to know if that's all right with you, mister. I guess you and the ladies and the youngsters had better get inside while I do it. It's a nasty business, but I guess it can't be helped."

There was a shocked silence.

Aunt Claire began to shoo Amanda and DeeDee into the house. Mrs. MacMinnies put her hands on her bony hips and pursed her mouth. But Amanda and DeeDee didn't budge. They stared wide-eyed at Mr. Bodine.

Amanda clutched at Uncle Oliver's sleeve.

"Did you hear him, Poppa?" she cried. "Can't you do something?"

"I heard him," Uncle Oliver said. His face glowed slowly red with outrage. He turned to Mr. Bodine.

"Why do you have to shoot her?" he asked at last. His voice was terribly calm.

Mr. Bodine shifted his weight from one foot to the other. "There's no other way, mister," he said.

"I see," said Uncle Oliver in that same dangerously quiet voice.

"I'll get my rifle now," Mr. Bodine said. He walked off toward his car.

Charlie Murofino said in a low tone, as though he was talking to himself, "Mrs. Houghton set great store by that dog. I remember when she bought her. It was just before I left to go into the navy. She paid a lot for her, too. Had the Kennel Club papers and all."

"How can you let him shoot her, Poppa?" Obie said tensely. "Maybe we could catch her later, when all the racket has died down. I bet I could collar her by myself, if nobody else was here."

Charlie shook his head. "You'll never get close enough to Maggie to grab her. She never would come near strangers. Mrs. Houghton was the only one she'd ever go to. I know she never let Barney Rudkin get within spitting range of her. He just set her food down and went away. Of course, Barney never was one to be patient with a dog, or with anything else for that matter."

Uncle Oliver's eyes narrowed as he stood there. He didn't say anything. And the collie watched us from the other side of the lane. She wasn't barking anymore, but her eyes were wary. You could see that she was ready to streak off again.

Mr. Bodine came back with his rifle.

We all held our breath.

Then Uncle Oliver said, "Just wait a minute before you—before you do it, would you?" He turned to Aunt Claire. He said in a low voice, "This is terrible, Claire. What do you think?"

Aunt Claire looked miserable. "I honestly don't know, Oliver," she answered. "It seems criminal to destroy the animal."

Then the explosion began. It was like a delayed bomb.

First of all, DeeDee began to bawl. You never heard such a clamor. Trust DeeDee. Still, this time it was in a good cause.

That got Amanda going. "Poppa," she said, and her face got all tight, like when she recites poetry, "you can't let him do it!"

And Obie, scowling, said, "Gosh, Poppa. She looks like a good dog. Don't let him shoot her!"

"If I don't shoot her," Mr. Bodine said, "she'll have to stay here. I can't spend any more time trying to catch her, and that's that."

Mrs. MacMinnies kept her lips pursed. "Sieglinde is quite enough dog for any one family," she remarked.

Amanda was looking more and more like Joan of Arc every second. "But Poppa, she belongs here. Walkaway Hill is her home!"

Then DeeDee really got to work. She turned on both faucets full blast.

"Mamma," she howled, "don't let that man kill her!" She clutched a wheezing, wriggling Sieglinde and stared up at her parents, fat tears rolling from those great big angel eyes of hers, and her lower lip quivering like Little Eva's. "Mamma," she quavered, "if I was to die, would you kill Sieglinde?"

Well, that did it.

Aunt Claire said hastily, "Why, dear, we'd do no such thing!"

Amanda and Obie had their eyes fixed accusingly on Uncle Oliver's face. DeeDee was regarding him as though he were the Lord High Executioner, or something.

Uncle Oliver's face became even more suffused with red than before. "Don't you look at me that way!" he said. He turned to Aunt Claire. "What do you say, Claire? Shall we let her hang around? Maybe she'll make a good watchdog."

"If anyone is asking me, which no one is," Mrs. MacMinnies put in, "that poor demented specimen wouldn't be much good for anything!"

"If we took care of her and loved her," Amanda said, "then maybe—"

"If!" snorted Mrs. MacMinnies. "If my grandmother had wheels she'd have been a bicycle."

"We can't just stand here and let her be killed in cold blood," Amanda said.

DeeDee only wailed louder.

Obie said, "After all, Poppa, she really has more right here than we have. We only bought the place. But she belongs here."

Mr. Bodine rubbed the barrel of his gun. "Well, mister, I guess it's up to you. Make up your mind. I got to get home before dark. What do you want me to do?"

"I think," said Uncle Oliver gravely, "that perhaps you'd better go along then and leave her here. This is her home. We'll keep her."

DeeDee stopped bawling at once. Amanda and Obie and I set up a cheer. Even Aunt Claire was smiling.

"All right, mister. Anything you say. It's your place now. But if you decide to change your mind later, call me up and I'll come and do the job for you."

"I don't think I'll change my mind," Uncle Oliver replied.

Mr. Bodine got into his car and drove away. Charlie waved after him, grinning.

The shaggy collie crouched in the tall dry grass, her muzzle resting on her forepaws, watching us. Her coat was almost indistinguishable from the dead stalks, but her ears were pricked up and alert. It was almost as though she understood what had happened. And she wasn't barking anymore.

Charlie Murofino turned to Uncle Oliver. "I'll dump that paint and the boy's valise now, Mr. Little. I'd better be getting home before the better half raises Cain. So long, all. See you tomorrow morning." He got the paint cans and my bag and set them on the porch. Then he called over to the collie, "Well, Maggie, you're safe now. I guess Walkaway Hill still belongs to you!" And off he went, still grinning.

"Maggie!" said Mrs. MacMinnies with a loud sniff. "That's no name for a dog."

Uncle Oliver remained silent. He seemed stunned by all that had happened.

"Well, Oliver?" Aunt Claire said.

"I never thought when I applied for the mortgage on this place," he observed wryly, "that I should have signed my name Farley Mowatt!" Then he seemed to notice me for the first time. "Well, James," he said, "now that that's settled, welcome to Walkaway Hill!"

4

THE WHITE ELEPHANT

Now that all that was settled I could take a good look at Walkaway Hill.

As I said before, it wasn't at all what I had expected. It wasn't a Stately Home or what the books call a Gem of Colonial Design. It was just a big white rambling house with jigsaw scrollwork around the porches and little bull's-eye attic windows under the pointed eaves. It didn't even look really old. It was more what I'd call elderly.

Furthermore, there was no denying that there was a definite air of neglect to Walkaway Hill. It was a little like Maggie in that respect. You felt that nobody had bothered to love it for a long time. I could see, too, what Charlie Murofino meant when he called it a white elephant. And yet I have to admit that I liked Walkaway Hill right from the start. I mean, it looked like the kind of place where you might find all sorts of unexpected things: hidden stairways and dark winding passages and secret rooms.

There was another thing about Walkaway Hill, something that, although we didn't realize it then, was going to make a difference to what happened later.

From where we stood you couldn't see a single sign of any other habitation. Even the road was well out of sight. Through the towering evergreens that surrounded the house the only things to be seen were the sloping fields, covered with a jungle of weeds, the bare trees of the encroaching woodlands, the barn and a few outbuildings; and then, in the distance, the spreading humps of the mountains. Now that Mr. Bodine and Charlie had driven away, everything was terribly quiet. You almost expected to hear a bat squeak. You couldn't even hear any cars passing on the road below us. The stillness was something you could have cut with a scout knife. And yet I couldn't help feeling that it was a living stillness. There was no telling what might come out of it. That was the exciting part.

Of course, I didn't have much time to get my bearings just then because greetings were in order. Everybody talked at once, but then it has always been a job getting in a word edgewise when the Littles are around. Obie and Amanda wanted to drag me off right away to explore. "There's a lot of wonderful old machinery kicking around in that barn," Obie was saying, "although I haven't really had a chance yet to look it over properly." And Amanda was all for taking me down to the pond that very instant. "James," she said, "it's the most romantic spot you ever saw. It's not so much a pond as a—as a tarn! It's exactly like something out of *Wuthering Heights*." *Wuthering Heights* was Amanda's favorite book at the moment and everything she saw reminded her of it.

DeeDee wanted to show me something else: I think it was the tree that was going to have real baby apples when the summer came. Anyway, I could tell that they were really excited about the place. What I wanted most of all right then was a conference with Obie and Amanda about what they had written in their letter. But I knew that it would have to wait until later.

Aunt Claire broke in gently, "James probably wants to see his room before he does anything else. And besides, it's too late for you to go wandering off. It'll be dark soon."

Obie said scornfully, "Who's afraid of the dark?"

Mrs. MacMinnies clapped her hands to her gray topknot. "And I've got supper going on the stove," she cried. "The dear knows, it's probably all burned to cinders by now!" And off she flew toward the kitchen.

So we went inside.

Obie helped me lug my suitcase upstairs, and Aunt Claire showed me my room. It was next to Obie's and across the hall from Amanda's, and it was a perfectly fine room. I mean, I liked it especially because it wasn't all gussied up as yet with curtains and rugs and all that sort of junk. It just had a cot in it and a table and a chair. In one corner there was a pile of stuff waiting to be unpacked.

Aunt Claire glanced dubiously around at the naked walls.

"I hope you'll be comfortable here, James," she said. "As you can see, we're still more or less camping out."

I told her that so far as I was concerned, everything was all right. I suppose she saw that I really meant it, because she bent impulsively and gave me a squeeze. "You're our very first guest at Walkaway Hill," she said. "I'm glad you're here, James."

I was saved from having to make any appropriate sappy response by Uncle Oliver's appearing in the doorway with DeeDee and Sieglinde trailing at his heels. Then Amanda dashed in with an armload of books. She dumped them on the bed. "I've brought you some of my special favorites. There's—"

"There will be time enough for all that later," Uncle Oliver interrupted. "Come along, James. Right now I'm going to take you on Squire Little's Official Guided Tour of the Premises."

"I'm coming too," said Amanda.

"So am I," Obie announced.

"Nobody's leaving me and Sieglinde out of anything!" DeeDee piped up, shaking those brass curls of hers. It was true enough. It's always been a job getting rid of DeeDee, especially when there's a real reason for not wanting her around.

Aunt Claire stood in the doorway as we all trooped after Uncle Oliver. I could see her trying not to smile.

Squire Little's Official Guided Tour started downstairs.

There's no need to go into a long description of everything. I think descriptions are pretty boring for the most part, anyway. But it was a real old-fashioned kind of house. I was sort of confused at first. Until I got used to the layout, everything was a regular maze. There were passages all over the place, and steps going up and down where you least expected them. The living room had a noble large fireplace, big enough to hold a barbecue in, and so did the dining room. The kitchen was the old farmhouse type they're always showing in advertisements, and it even had an enormous coal range, in addition to the electric stove. Mrs. MacMinnies had already polished it so that it gleamed like a monument to the heroes of the Spanish-American War.

Mrs. MacMinnies surveyed it as though it were her most prized possession.

"We'll probably never use the thing," Amanda said.

"Never you mind," snapped Mrs. MacMinnies ominously. "You never can tell what might happen in the country."

We all looked very superior at that, Uncle Oliver most of all. But then, the chief trouble with Mrs. MacMinnies is that she usually turns out to be right. Not always, but at least eight times out of ten.

Beyond the kitchen there were all sorts of passages. One of them led to a kind of workshop, another took you out to what Mrs. MacMinnies referred to as "my cold larder," and at the far end of that a creaking door opened on to a woodshed. Sieglinde, who had been following us, panting and wheezing every step of the way, now stood stock-still and whined.

Mrs. MacMinnies glanced bleakly over our shoulders at the dark, damp-smelling piles of logs and old lumber.

"It's probably full of rats," said she, sniffing in disdain.

Obie's eyes brightened.

"Do you really think so?" he said.

"Ugh," she answered with a shudder. "It wouldn't surprise me atall no matter what came out of there. Spiders and whatnot. I'll thank all of you to keep that door shut."

We went back to the kitchen, where Sieglinde collapsed under the table. Nothing could budge her. I guess what with the queer smells in the woodshed competing with the familiar smell of dinner, it was all too much for her. And, since it was Sieglinde, dinner won.

Uncle Oliver waved us back to the hall, taking great

pains meanwhile to point out everything. "Just look at those floorboards!" I looked at them, and to tell the truth they didn't seem any different from any other floorboards I'd seen. But there was no sense hurting his feelings, so I admired them all the same. Aunt Claire, who was coming down the stairs just then with an armful of curtains and towels, said, "You mustn't mind your Uncle Oliver, James. He's as proud of this place as though he'd built every inch of it himself." And I guess he was.

I must admit that the house wouldn't have suited everyone, but I could see it was all right for the Littles. Of course, even I could tell there was still lots of work to be done. Everywhere you looked there were signs of neglect, like peeling wallpaper and little cracks across the corners of windowpanes. And the floors were stacked with boxes that were still waiting to be unpacked.

"You have no idea, James, of the rubbish we had to cart out of here," Uncle Oliver said. "It was pretty grim at first, I'll admit, but it's taking shape. It's all taking shape." He looked around, and there was a flicker of real satisfaction behind his horn-rimmed glasses. In fact, the living room was already pretty much the way it was going to be, and so were the kitchen and the dining room. Most of the downstairs had been given a fresh coat of paint—that was Charlie Murofino's contribution. "I don't mind telling you, James, that we've all worked like stevedores."

"*We* have," put in Obie. "You just stood around telling us what to do."

"It was not an easy task exercising my executive capacities with this crew," replied Uncle Oliver with considerable dignity.

Obie snorted.

Uncle Oliver looked hurt.

"Never mind, Poppa," Obie said kindly.

Then we went upstairs. I didn't think there was anything very special about it—it was all bedrooms—until we came to a door at the end of the hall.

"And now, James," Uncle Oliver resumed in an impressive voice, "permit me to usher you into the sanctum sanctorum, which is Latin for Officers' Country."

I figured it was just going to be another bedroom, but when he pushed the door open, I really got a tremendous surprise.

"Well, James, what do you think of this?"

"Wow!" I said. There was nothing else to say.

It was the biggest and best room in the whole house. It was just about as high as it was wide, and all across one end there were huge windows facing on the woods behind the house. Uncle Oliver's books were piled in the middle of the floor, but his desk and his typewriter and his filing cabinets were already set in place. On a shelf behind the desk was a complete set of the Hal Sterling books.

"It used to be Mrs. Houghton's studio," Uncle Oliver said. "But it's mine now. I've always wanted a room like this to work in. The books'll really come pouring out now." He looked as happy as a kid with a new set of electric trains.

"Hal Sterling rides again!" Obie said under his breath in a snide sort of way.

"What was that?" Uncle Oliver asked, fixing Obie with a glance.

"Nothing, Poppa," said Obie with a grin.

"Well, James, that's it. Now you've seen it all," Uncle Oliver announced, shooting another suspicious glance in Obie's direction. Obie just looked blank.

Out in the hall, as we were leaving the studio, I noticed something odd in the ceiling. It was a cord that dangled from one end of a sort of wooden frame.

"What's that?" I demanded.

"Oh, it just leads up to the attic," Uncle Oliver replied. He yanked at the cord and a trapdoor swung down toward us. There was a set of folding steps attached to it.

"What's up there?"

"Just junk. We've got to clear it all out one of these days when I'm feeling ambitious."

"Can't James see it now, Poppa?"

"Not now. There's no light up there. And besides, tomorrow's another day," Uncle Oliver added firmly.

I couldn't help sighing enviously. "Gosh," I said, as Uncle Oliver sent the trapdoor swinging back into place, "this house has everything!"

"Just about," Uncle Oliver agreed proudly. "There's only one thing missing."

"What's that, Poppa?" Obie asked.

Uncle Oliver's eyes twinkled behind his glasses.

"A ghost," he said with a chuckle.

Obie snorted again.

"I wish we had a ghost!" Amanda cried. "Then it would be exactly like *Wuthering Heights*."

"We can't have everything," Uncle Oliver said. "Maybe when we get the house all paid for—if we ever do—we can buy a modest little specter on the installment plan. We might even look them up after supper in the Sears catalogue. And now I think I can hear something that sounds very much like one, only it's only Mrs. MacMinnies, howling in her usual banshee fashion. What's she saying, Amanda?"

"I think it's something about washing our hands for dinner."

"Then the tour is officially over."

"All the same," said Amanda thoughtfully as we pelted downstairs, "I wish we did have a ghost."

Which was very prophetic of Amanda.

5

ONE THIRD OF
A GHOST

Mrs. MacMinnies produced one of her usual sumptuous repasts. In addition to the roast beef and vegetables there were popovers with jelly, and we had floating island for dessert. "Only everything tastes better than ever, doesn't it, James, because we're in our own house now!" Amanda exclaimed.

Mrs. MacMinnies only said, "Don't talk with your mouth full, Amanda. It's not ladylike," and stalked out of the dining room to fetch more popovers. Mrs. MacMinnies is like that. She enjoys compliments but she doesn't like to admit it.

Every so often during the meal we could catch a glimpse of Maggie through the uncurtained windows. She kept circling the house uneasily, but she was quiet now. There was no more of that Hound of the Baskervilles stuff, which I don't mind admitting was a relief.

Obie said, half rising from his chair, "I guess she's hungry."

Aunt Claire fixed him with a stern matriarchal eye.

"Mrs. MacMinnies will feed her after supper," she said. She turned to me. "We haven't fed her before, James," she explained. "I suppose it sounds heartless, but you see, we were expecting them to come and get her every day. It seemed wrong to have her get attached to us only to be taken away."

"I think it was mean," Amanda said, her eyes flashing. Amanda hates injustice, especially where animals are concerned. I remember how she cried all the way through *Black Beauty*. As a matter of fact, I nearly did too, but that was two years ago, when I was a lot younger than I am now.

"It would have been much meaner," Uncle Oliver put in, "for the benighted beast to get used to us, and then, the minute she felt secure and trustful, to have Mr. Bodine remove her from the property."

When supper was over, Amanda and Obie and I raced into the kitchen. Mrs. MacMinnies was fixing Sieglinde's dinner, while Sieglinde stood underfoot, practically slavering.

"What about Maggie?" Obie said.

"I don't play favorites here," Mrs. MacMinnies said. "She'll have hers too." She filled a second bowl with scraps.

"I'll give it to her," Obie said.

"Can't I, Mrs. MacMinnies?" Amanda pleaded.

And then DeeDee appeared.

She turned those great big blue accusing eyes on us.

"You were going to feed Maggie, weren't you?"

"The creature's been elected a member of the Little

family," Mrs. MacMinnies observed acidly, "so she might as well be fed like the rest."

"Let me!" DeeDee cried. "Let me feed her!" She looked dangerously close to another flood, so Mrs. MacMinnies without a word handed the bowl to her.

DeeDee went out with it to the porch. Through the window we could see Maggie moving through the evening shadows, barking at DeeDee, but she wouldn't come near her, not even when she held out the bowl.

"Just set it down and leave it be," Mrs. MacMinnies called through the window. "She'll come and eat it if she's hungry. If not, it won't be the first time Sieglinde's had more than she needed."

Reluctantly, DeeDee put the bowl on the porch floor and backed inside. We watched the dog look nervously around. She edged toward the bowl, sniffed at it cautiously, and then shied away. She did this several times. Then one of us happened to budge. She darted off as though she'd been shot.

"She'll never touch it while you're all crowded there at the window like a busload of tourists at the zoo," Mrs. MacMinnies said.

So we went away from the window and helped Mrs. MacMinnies do the dishes.

Suddenly DeeDee let out a screech.

I nearly dropped a platter.

"Look! She's eating!"

It was true enough. Maggie was wolfing the food as though it was the first decent meal she'd ever had. We watched tensely while she licked the bowl spotless. Even Mrs. MacMinnies seemed touched. "Poor thing!" she exclaimed. "She could do with a bit of spoiling, not like some dogs I could mention," and she glanced down at Sieglinde, sleek and full to bursting, wriggling ingratiatingly by the table in the hope of getting a few choice dividends. "Out with you, now!" Mrs. MacMinnies commanded.

She opened the door and Sieglinde waddled into the night air. Then Sieglinde stood perfectly still while Maggie came over to her and sniffed.

DeeDee asked anxiously, "Are they going to fight?"

"Wait and see," Obie said gruffly, but I could tell he was worried. I was, too, for that matter.

There was a great deal of sniffing back and forth after that. Sieglinde got up on her hind legs, with her forepaws on Maggie's chest. They just reached. And then, to our astonishment, Maggie began to wag her tail. Sieglinde's was already going so fast, I thought it would snap off.

"Do you think they're going to be friends now?" DeeDee asked, wide-eyed.

"Why not?" Amanda said.

DeeDee looked thoughtful.

Then, "But how can each of them tell that the other's a dog too?" she piped. "I mean, they look so different."

They did, too. Maggie, powerful and wild, with her lion's mane and great waving tail, was big enough for Sieglinde to waddle right under her. Sieglinde's fur was short and glossy and sleek, like a lady's expensive coat, while Maggie's was more like a ragbag than anything. They didn't really look as though they belonged to the same species.

Obie scratched his chin. "I guess they just know," he said. "That's all there is to it."

Maggie dashed off into the darkness of the lane, Sieglinde trotting after her as best she could on those short legs of hers, her tail still going like anything.

"Well," Amanda exclaimed. "Who would have thought

that fat selfish old Sieglinde would have turned out to be so sociable?"

Later, we tried to get Maggie to come into the house. Coax as we might, she wouldn't come within yards of any of us. She wouldn't even approach the porch so long as someone was out on it. And yet it seemed as though she knew that she was already part of the Little family. She no longer barked when she saw us. That, we figured, was progress of a sort. And when it was time for Sieglinde to come indoors, we had to call and call before the dachshund would appear. Even then, she came reluctantly, as though she would much rather have remained outside, tagging after her new friend. You would have thought, from the way she stuck to the collie, that she had decided she was the big shaggy dog's queer-shaped shadow. And once inside, she kept looking toward the window and whining.

Well, before we knew it, it was time to go to bed.

Amanda whispered to me, "Let's have a General Convocation in my room as soon as the coast is clear. You pass the word on to Obie."

"Right," I said. "I can't wait to hear about what you wrote in the letter."

"The letter?" She giggled. "Oh James, that was just bait to get you up here right away. You're so detective-minded, I was sure it would work."

I was indignant. "You mean it was all a lie?"

She hesitated. "Well, not exactly. We did see some-thing mysterious out there between the trees one night."

"What do you mean, something mysterious?"

She frowned. "Obie and I were together when I saw it. I was sure it was there: a sort of hooded figure. It looked as though it was sneaking out of the house. But we decided afterward that it was just the shadows of the big

— 39 —

trees. And then, another time, there were some ominous footsteps."

"Amanda, are you telling the truth?"

"Of course I am. I was sure I heard them out on the porch. But Obie said I was just imagining things, that I just want everything to be like *Wuthering Heights* all the time." She sighed. "I suppose Obie was right."

"Oh," I said. It was really very crushing after all the high hopes I'd had.

"Anyway," Amanda said, "you will come to the Convocation?"

"All right," I said. "But I'm too sleepy for a pillow fight."

"Pillow fights!" Amanda said with a sniff. "They're infantile." She looked inscrutable. "I have a better idea."

"What?"

"Wait and see."

So when we'd brushed our teeth and gotten into our pajamas, Obie and I convened in Amanda's room as quietly as we could. We didn't want any grown-ups to interfere with remarks about how late it was, etc., etc. But even more than that, we didn't want DeeDee to find out that she was being left out of something. There'd have been the very dickens to pay if that had happened.

Amanda was sitting cross-legged on her bed. She had draped an old sweater over the lampshade so that the chamber was shrouded in appropriate murk.

"Hurry up and shut the door behind you," she said.

Obie closed the door noiselessly.

"All right, Amanda," he said. "What's on your mind?"

She narrowed her eyes in a way I hadn't seen since the time she had decided for a whole week that she was Morgan le Fay.

"Well," she said, slowly and deliberately. "I've been thinking."

"Big deal," said Obie. "Did it hurt?"

Amanda ignored that. "I've been thinking that now that we live here in the country it's going to be a lot different from New York. I mean, we're not going to miss being in the city, except for you, James. But we won't be having the same kind of adventures we had there. So I thought that if we organized a sort of secret society with just the three of us, we wouldn't miss James so much. We could correspond about the society and all that."

"What kind of secret society?" Obie demanded. Then he added suspiciously, "I suppose you'll be president."

"There doesn't have to be a president," Amanda said. "We wouldn't necessarily need one."

"I never heard of a society without a president," Obie retorted hotly. The real point, of course, is that Obie likes being president of things.

"Then ours will be the first. Listen. I propose that we form a society and that it be called the Wuthering Heights Society."

Obie looked scornful.

"And what would be the use of that?"

"It would be simply terrific! We could do all the things they do in the book. We could tramp over the moors and—well, and things like that."

"There aren't any moors around Walkaway Hill," Obie told her.

"We could find some if we looked hard enough. It would be very spooky and dramatic. And I'd be Heathcliff."

"I thought I smelled a rat," said Obie.

"You can't be Heathcliff, Amanda," I declared. "You're a girl."

"I made up the society and I should think I could be anyone that I chose in it," Amanda retorted. She looked out darkly at us from under her thatch of hair.

Obie and I exchanged a glance.

Then Obie said with a shrug, "Go ahead, James. You tell her."

"Well, Amanda," I said, girding my loins so to speak, "Wuthering Heights is out. I don't think it's such a hot idea and neither does Obie."

Amanda hates being overruled.

"Does either of you have a better one?" she flashed.

Obie sat quietly on the floor. He was thinking hard.

"Look here," he said suddenly. "The secret society idea is fine, and I think it ought to be spooky too. I like spooky things. Only I think it has to be based on something better than a book."

Amanda was considerably miffed at that.

"Of course," she said, "if you're better than Emily Brontë at thinking things up, go right ahead. I won't interfere. How can I? I'm only a girl, and it's two against one."

Obie stared at the ceiling fixture and I did my tension exercises with my toes, trying to think of something better than old Emily Brontë. Then I had my idea.

"We could be roving detectives and track down criminals!"

"What kinds of criminals?" Amanda demanded.

"All kinds, but mostly desperate ones. And we could collect the rewards if we found any of the ones they have on the posters in the post office."

Amanda shook her head.

"It's all right for you, James. You're still in New York.

Where are we going to find any criminals on Walkaway Hill?"

"Oh," I said. "I hadn't thought of that."

Then Obie emerged from his deep trance. His eyes had a very bright light in them, like a room in which somebody has just snapped on the electric switch.

"Listen to me, you two," he said. "What's the spookiest thing you know of?"

Amanda answered like a shot. "Edgar Allan Poe."

"Not books, lardhead," Obie said. "I mean, really the spookiest thing there is."

"Ghosts," I said at once. Amanda said it at the same time.

"Right!" said Obie triumphantly.

"Well?" Amanda said.

Slowly, in a low creepy voice, Obie announced, "Then why don't we form a Ghostly Society?"

I was stunned.

So was Amanda.

Obie went on, "Amanda always wants to play Ghost, the spelling kind, and I hate that because James is the only one of us who can spell, and we're always squabbling over who's supposed to be one third of a ghost. But this is a better way of playing Ghost. This way we can be one third of a ghost and all together we could be the whole ghost. Then, when the three of us are together, it would be a Ghostly Gathering."

I thought it was a great idea and said so at once.

Amanda considered. Amanda can be pretty irritating when she wants to be.

"I suppose it might conceivably work out," she said. "but what would be the purpose of it?"

"It would make more sense than a Wuthering Heights Society," Obie said flatly. "We could tell ghost stories, and look for vampires, and keep a pet bat and meet in deserted cemeteries, and—"

"And what else, might I ask?" a voice suddenly said out of the gloom.

We jumped, all three of us. Amanda's face was like a glass of milk. The voice intoned,

> *"From goblins and ghosties,*
> *And long-legged beasties,*
> *And things that go bump in the night,*
> *The good Lord preserve us!"*

I could feel my flesh creep along my bones.

And then we saw Mrs. MacMinnies standing in the doorway.

"Oh," said Amanda, "it's you." But she was relieved. So was Obie. And so, to tell the truth, was I.

"I suspected something unholy would be going on, with the three of you together again," said Mrs. Mac-Minnies. "Ghosts and vampires and cemeteries indeed!" She crossed herself. "God between us and all harm!" she breathed fervently.

Amanda said, "Do you actually believe in ghosts, Mrs. MacMinnies?"

"Don't be foolish, child."

"That's no answer. Do you believe in them, really?"

"No. But that doesn't mean I haven't got sense enough to be afraid of them. Now get to bed, the lot of you, before I call the mister and tell him what you've been up to."

"But Mrs. MacMinnies—"

Mrs. MacMinnies said nothing. She just pointed at the door.

And that was the end of our Convocation. But it was

nothing near the last of the Gathering of Ghosts at Walkaway Hill.

Obie and I scuttled back to our rooms. I slept like a rock for a long time. I'm not sure how long, though, because in the middle of the night I suddenly woke up scared, and not knowing why.

I huddled among the blankets and listened. I could hear the shutters banging against the side of the house. The March wind was whistling. It sounded shrill and almost human. and then, over everything else, I could make out Maggie's wild barking. I couldn't help it. It sent shivers down my back.

After that I lay in the dark, listening and trying not to imagine things. I remembered what Charlie Murofino had told me about Mrs. Houghton, and I couldn't sleep. I know it sounds silly. I mean, it was only Maggie, after all. But there was something about that barking that really set your teeth on edge. It was worse than a fork scraping against the side of a pot: that, and the wind, and the shutters that wouldn't stop banging. Through the curtainless window I could see the black branches whipping around outside. I got up and looked out. I could see Maggie's shaggy silhouette. She was running like a haunted thing, her head raised; and that weird barking went on and on. It wouldn't stop. I couldn't help feeling that something was wrong. It was as though some unaccounted-for presence really was abroad on Walkaway Hill.

I wished we hadn't talked about ghosts. I was ready to believe in them myself right then. In fact, for a moment I was almost convinced that the shaggy collie was the ghost of the lately departed Mrs. Houghton.

Barefoot, I padded into Obie's room. He was on his back, his arms flung up over his head as though somebody had just said, "Reach for it!" and he was smiling in his sleep. The floor was icy and I sneezed, but Obie didn't even stir. He just lay there and enjoyed his dream. So I crept back to my room and dived onto the cot.

I covered my head with the blankets, shoved the pillow on top of them, and tried not to listen or think or anything.

And then, eventually, I fell asleep again.

The next thing I knew, daylight was streaming over my face and Obie was flicking the end of a towel at my feet where they stuck out from under the scrunched-up bedclothes.

"Come on, James," he shouted. "Get up, for Pete's sake. We've got the whole place to explore."

I blinked.

Everything was just as usual, and the pleasant smell of Mrs. MacMinnies's flapjacks and sausages curled up the stairs from the kitchen.

But as I washed and dressed, I still had the uneasy feeling that I'd heard at least one third of a ghost haunting Walkaway Hill during the night.

6

SIEGLINDE

By the time Obie and I got downstairs, the house was already jumping. Aunt Claire and Uncle Oliver had finished their breakfast and were carting things out of the main hall.

"Good morning," Aunt Claire called. "Did you sleep well, James?"

I was about to make some kind of noncommittal answer, when I realized that she was too wrapped up in what Uncle Oliver was doing to attend to anything I'd say. I've noticed that half the time so-called adults ask questions, they're not really interested in the answers; and that when you ask them questions, they're just as likely not to be interested in answering. This is a very significant point. As for Uncle Oliver, he was carrying a large oil painting into the living room. Between puffs he muttered something about being "bowed by the weight of centuries." Then we heard him grunt, and I couldn't be sure if it was supposed to be a greeting or a protest at the weight of the frame on that family portrait.

We picked our way over the piled-up stuff and went into the kitchen. Mrs. MacMinnies, in a starched apron that was so crisp, it practically rattled, bustled between the stove and the refrigerator. DeeDee and Amanda were already at the table, gulping orange juice. Amanda had her usual tousled morning look: her hair hanging in hanks on either side of her face. She wore an old sweater and a pair of blue jeans that looked as though they'd barely managed to come through the Battle of Gettysburg, and she had a book propped up against the salt shaker, only it kept slipping. DeeDee, of course, was as neat as a baby movie star, with every metallic curl in place. She positively reeked.

"She's been at the vanilla extract again," Mrs. MacMinnies announced.

DeeDee smirked. "I like to smell nice," she said.

Sieglinde as usual was underfoot, squirming and whining. She didn't seem to be at all interested in the bits of breakfast that DeeDee slipped to her under the table, which for Sieglinde was a wonder. She kept rolling her eyes toward the door.

"I think Sieglinde's sick," DeeDee announced as Obie and I took our places at the kitchen table.

"Sick my sainted foot," said Mrs. MacMinnies.

"Well," DeeDee persisted, "something's the matter with her."

Mrs. MacMinnies favored Sieglinde with one of her withering glances.

"If you ask me, she just wants to be let out again."

"But she hasn't even had her breakfast yet," DeeDee declared.

"I don't care what she hasn't had. Open the door for her," Mrs. MacMinnies commanded.

DeeDee tossed her head. She slid off her chair and opened the kitchen door. In no time at all, and with a speed that knocked every one of us for a loop, Sieglinde hurled herself across the porch and was under the trees where Maggie lay staring distrustfully over Walkaway Hill. Sieglinde greeted the shaggy collie as though Maggie were her dearest friend, long lost to her.

Obie whistled through his teeth.

"Can you beat that!" he exclaimed. "She wouldn't even wait until after breakfast. It's just not the same old Sieglinde."

We watched the two of them go through an elaborate ritual of sniffing. Then they pattered off down the lane.

Amanda giggled.

"They look so funny together," she said, "as though Maggie were like Sieglinde's governess—a little mad, of course, but such a gentlewoman all the same!"

DeeDee just scowled over the rim of her glass. I could tell she was feeling pouty because that fat dog of hers would rather go off and run with Maggie than stay beside DeeDee's chair drooling for scraps.

"I don't care what Sieglinde does," DeeDee said, which was a whopping lie.

"There's juice in that pitcher," Mrs. MacMinnies announced. "You boys can get it for yourselves. And as soon as you've had it, your griddle cakes'll be ready."

The orange juice was cold enough to make your teeth chatter, and the griddle cakes were wonderful. I waited until we were on our seconds. Then, very casually, I asked, "Did anyone hear anything last night?"

DeeDee said balefully, "I heard you and Obie talking in Amanda's room."

We all ignored that.

"Hear anything? Like what?" Obie wanted to know.

"Like nothing special," I said. "Just anything."

Obie looked blank, which was no surprise to me, considering the way he slept. He'd have snored his way through a typhoon.

Amanda said, "The only thing I heard was the wind. It sounded terribly romantic."

"Just like *Wuthering Heights*, I suppose," said Obie with a snicker.

"As a matter of fact, it was, exactly," Amanda answered defiantly.

"And was that all?" I asked.

"Except for Maggie's barking," Amanda added. "But I've sort of gotten used to that. She's been barking ever since we got here."

Mrs. MacMinnies placed her hands on her hips and stared in a brooding way out of the window at the gray weather.

"I wish I could hear something," she said. "This business of living in the middle of nowhere may be all right for some, but it makes me jumpy. It's so quiet and all. I miss the traffic. Even a few trucks roaring along in the night would be more music to my ears than John McCormack singing 'The Rose of Tralee.'"

"Why, Mrs. MacMinnies," Obie said gallantly, "we'll make as much noise for you as you want."

"Never you mind," said she to that.

"But I thought you lived on a farm when you were a girl in Ireland," Amanda said thoughtfully.

Mrs. MacMinnies drew herself up.

"I was not born in Ireland, I was born in Liverpool. We were Liverpool Irish, not bog Irish, I'll have you know, and the only land we ever owned was what was in our window boxes. As a matter of fact, I'm really Scotch-Irish. My Pa and Ma were Irish, and the late Mr. MacMinnies, God rest his soul, was Scotch. That makes me Scotch-Irish."

"Oh," said Obie. We'd all heard that part of it before, and knew that it was senseless to argue about it.

As though I wasn't really thinking of anything in particular, I went on: "I wonder what it was that Maggie could have been barking at."

Amanda replied, "It's just the way Maggie is, James. She probably thought she was protecting us."

"That doesn't sound right," I said.

"That blessed dog!" Mrs. MacMinnies gave a loud and disdainful sniff. "She's so queer she'd bark at a leaf. And now," she said, "I hope you're all finished for this morning. I can't stay here the whole immortal day dishing out food. I've other things to do with my time."

"Like what?" Amanda said.

"Never you mind, Miss Pert. Skedaddle now, the lot of you." She cocked her head to one side. "There, that creature's at it again, barking at nothing."

"But dogs don't bark at nothing," I protested.

She peered through the window. "Well, I see it's that painter man coming up the lane this time, so if you want to devil somebody you can go and be the botheration of him."

There was no mistaking the rattle of Charlie Murofino's pickup truck as it approached the house.

Mrs. MacMinnies shook her head. "He's the skinny one, though! No more meat on him than you'd find on a picked bone. It's my notion that wife of his doesn't feed him enough. Lots of potatoes and gravy, that's what he needs."

"Anyway, Mrs. MacMinnies," I said pleasantly, "you'd make a wonderful wife."

She froze me with a cold eye. "I had no complaints from Mr. MacMinnies while he was alive, may the dear man rest in peace."

"I only meant that it was a good breakfast you gave us," I said hastily.

"I'll have none of your blarneying, now, James," she answered with a toss of her head. "I'm on to your tricks. You're as bad as a born Paddy with that complimenting tongue of yours." But I could tell she was pleased.

We pelted out to the hall to greet Charlie. He had a white painter's cap stuck on top of his black crew cut and he carried a bright red dinner pail.

"Morning, all," he said. He jerked his thumb in the direction of the lane. "I see those two are getting along all right. That sausage hound of yours is sticking to Maggie like a leech."

"Sieglinde," said DeeDee coldly, "is not a sausage hound. She is a purebred pedigreed dachshund."

"Fancy that, now," Charlie said with a wink at the rest of us. "I guess I must be losing my eyesight. I could have sworn she was one of those old-fashioned sauerkraut-and-sausage hounds. Well, I'll see you later. I've got to start slapping paint onto this wall. How about getting some of those boxes out of my way?"

Well, we never got around to doing any exploring that morning. We all moved furniture and cartons until our arms ached. The tiredness in the small of the back was the worst of it. And then, before we knew it, lunchtime had caught up with us.

Charlie set down his brush, stepped back, and surveyed the hall. It looked pretty dazzling.

"Notice any holidays?"

"Holidays?"

"Sure. Places I've missed."

We looked, but we couldn't find any.

"I thought not," he said with a satisfied nod. He picked up his fire truck–colored dinner pail and marched out to the porch with it.

Then Aunt Claire came and announced that Mrs. MacMinnies had been too busy to do any more than make a lot of sandwiches for us. "There's plenty of milk, and the cookie jar is at least half full, so that ought to do you."

"Can we take ours out on the porch and eat with Charlie?" Amanda asked.

"I don't see why not," Aunt Claire said, "if you all put sweaters and coats on. It seems to be getting colder."

"Wait for us, Charlie!" Obie called. "We're coming out too."

Amanda lost no time loading a tray for the rest of us. I could see that DeeDee was torn between eating like a grown-up and trailing after us. It didn't take much figuring to know that in the end she'd come outside. If there's anyone new around, DeeDee never rests until she's made a conquest, which is one of the reasons she's such a nuisance. She was glad to have a chance to fascinate Charlie, but she remained sort of sulky because Sieglinde hadn't been near her all morning. That perambulating frankfurter was still panting around after Maggie.

"What do you think they find to do together?" she asked Obie.

"Oh," said Obie, "they just like to sniff around the place."

Sure enough, when we went out to sit with Charlie on the porch steps, there on the other side of the lane was

Maggie, snuffling through the dead leaves, with Sieglinde doing her best to keep up with her.

"Sieglinde! You come here right this minute!" DeeDee called. But Sieglinde paid no attention. DeeDee waved her sandwich. Sieglinde still just kept going after Maggie as though her life depended on it. She went in circles, and she was letting out high excited yips.

Obie laughed. "Sieglinde looks just like a tugboat chasing after an ocean liner."

"You can say that again," Charlie said, smiling.

Then Obie was struck by a sudden thought. He turned to Charlie. "What do you suppose Maggie lived on all that time?" he asked.

Charlie took another swig of coffee from his thermos flask.

"All what time?" he asked.

"You know. All the time when nobody was around to feed her."

Charlie shrugged. "Rabbits and such," he said. "Small game. Whatever she could catch. I guess she made out. Of course," he added, "collies aren't real hunters."

"Aren't they?"

He shook his head. "Not much nose," he said. "But they have keen sight and they can move fast when they want to."

We all looked at Maggie with new interest.

Amanda said, sighing, "Poor rabbits!" Amanda is very tenderhearted.

Charlie's smile broadened to a grin.

"You won't say that once you've started your garden. Rabbits look cute and all that, but they can really raise hob among growing vegetables. You'll be glad of Maggie then, to keep down the population." Charlie glanced over at Sieglinde and eyed her speculatively. "Now, that dog of yours," he said, "ought to be a real hunter."

We all laughed, except DeeDee.

"Sieglinde?" Obie yelled in delighted astonishment.

Charlie nodded quite seriously. "That's what they're raised for," he said. "Dachshund—that's German for badger hound. They bred them low-slung that way so that they could work their way into badger holes. And those powerful short paws of theirs, they're for digging after the old badger when he retreats. Yep," said Charlie, "they're real hunters and no mistake."

Obie scratched his ear. "Well, who'd have thought it," he said. "Fat old Sieglinde!"

DeeDee, for once, said nothing. She just regarded Sieglinde openmouthed.

Then Amanda broke in. "Charlie—I mean, Mr. Murofino—tell us about Walkaway Hill. I mean, how it was before we came."

"I guess you mean about Mrs. Houghton."

Amanda nodded and passed him a cookie.

"Well," Charlie began slowly, "it's hard to tell about her."

"Didn't she have any children?"

"Nope. She didn't have anyone. She was a widow, and it looks as though she didn't have a single soul left that was related to her. Maybe that's why she thought so much about Maggie, not having any people to belong to her, I mean."

Amanda nodded gravely. She stared out at Walkaway Hill, at the trees and the outbuildings and the mountains that ringed it all, and she said, "It's so strange to think of this place with no children on it. It seems such a waste."

"Well," said Charlie, "that's the way it was."

"Did she live here a long time?" Obie inquired.

"Longer than I know about. Twenty, thirty years at least, it must have been."

DeeDee piped up shrilly, "Did she have lots and lots of party dresses?"

"DeeDee!" Amanda said, disgusted.

"I don't care, that's what I want to know about," DeeDee insisted.

But Charlie answered as though DeeDee's question was as good as anyone else's.

"She never spent much on her clothes, though I suppose she could have if she'd wanted to. You wouldn't think she was anybody, just to look at her."

Amanda knitted her brows.

"Was she a nice person?" she asked at last.

"That's hard to answer. She wasn't easy to get along with, if that's what you mean by nice." He closed his eyes for a second. Then he said, "I'd say she was interesting. If you rubbed her the right way, that is. She had a sharp tongue, and what she said had a real twist to it sometimes—if it wasn't aimed at you. And she had pretty definite ideas about everything. Wouldn't put up with this or that. Knew just where she stood about religion and politics and all. Didn't care for back talk, either. Like I was telling James here, yesterday, sooner or later she quarreled with everybody she knew. Finally it got so she didn't have anyone left but Maggie. Except for Barney Rudkin, that is. And he wasn't much."

"Barney Rudkin?" Obie and Amanda said it at the same time. I saw that Charlie had never gotten around to telling them about him. "Who was Barney Rudkin?"

"Well," Charlie said, reflecting, "that's a good question.

"Like I said, it got to the point where Mrs. Houghton couldn't get anybody to stay on the place. It was mostly the ladies she couldn't get on with. When I worked for her, everything went fine until I got married. Then she tangled with the missus. She had the Van Sicklens for a while. But sure enough, the time came when Emma Van Sicklen wouldn't stay another minute because of something Mrs. Houghton said to her. I think it was about not putting too much sugar in the raspberry preserves, or like that. Well, the Van Sicklens left, and they were sort of the bottom of the barrel. And of course the place had to be kept up. She was very particular about certain things: the wood to be cut and stacked for the fireplaces, and the barn, even though there wasn't any stock in it anymore. She was fussy about the orchard, too. And she didn't drive, so she needed someone to chauffeur her around. And then there were the bees to be looked after."

"Bees?" Obie asked excitedly.

DeeDee looked around with apprehension.

"Yep, bees. But I'll tell you about them later. Are there any more of those cookies left? Well, as I was saying, there she was, all alone again, marooned like a rock at high tide, and no one to take her shopping or look after the place for her. That was when Barney Rudkin came along.

"No one knew where she picked him up in the first place. And no one liked him much, either. Oh, he was a glib enough talker, but he had a surly way with him underneath. I guess he knew how to handle the old lady, though. Or else he knew she'd had it if he went. And maybe he figured he was on to a good thing, because he stayed. I don't think he liked it when the place was sold. I guess he'd counted on staying on."

"Which was his room?" Amanda asked.

"His room?" said Charlie. "Oh, Barney didn't sleep in

the big house. He bunked down in what we used to call the honey house."

"The honey house?"

Charlie waved at one of the outbuildings. We could just glimpse it through the trees. It was really more of a shack than anything. "That's it, over there. It's where all the stuff for the beehives used to be kept. I'll show it to you later, if you like."

"Show it to us now!" DeeDee said.

"Can't."

"Why not?"

"Because I've got to get back on the job now, that's why. But I'll show you after I knock off for the day."

"You won't forget, Charlie?" Obie said.

"I won't forget."

"The honey house!" Amanda breathed dreamily.

Just then Uncle Oliver stuck his head out through the door.

"Finished your lunch?"

We all nodded.

"Then how about marching down to the mailbox to see if there's any word from the outer world?"

Obie said sure, we'd be glad to.

"I'm going back inside with Charlie," DeeDee announced.

Charlie tucked his empty thermos flask back into his dinner pail, put the pail on the seat of his truck, and went to inspect his brushes. We started off down the lane. Obie whistled for the dogs. Sieglinde came waddling along after us, and Maggie shadowed us from a safe distance. Sieglinde kept looking around to make sure that the big dog was following. Obie didn't say anything, but I knew he was feeling set up because they were tagging along.

Then, at the top of the lane, at the halfway point where it dips and goes down, Maggie stopped and wouldn't go any farther.

Sieglinde stopped too.

"Come on, Sieglinde!"

She wouldn't move.

She looked at us and then at Maggie. Then she trotted back and stood in the middle of the lane. Maggie stood over her protectively.

"Come on, Sieglinde!" we called. We even started running downhill, but Sieglinde wouldn't budge her fat self from Maggie's shadow. She planted her hindquarters firmly on the ground and rolled up her eyes adoringly at Maggie.

When we came back from the mailbox, there she was, waiting right there with the collie.

Both of them were watching us, but neither of them moved. It was as though Sieglinde were waiting for Maggie to give her the signal before she'd stir a paw.

"You know," Amanda said, "I think Sieglinde's decided that she belongs to Maggie now. She thinks she's Maggie's dog!"

And to tell the truth, it did look as though Sieglinde were already Maggie's, body and soul, and glad to be.

Obie scratched his ear thoughtfully. Then he let out a hoot.

"I don't think DeeDee is going to like this one bit!"

7

TWO THIRDS OF
A GHOST

Mrs. MacMinnies is always saying, "There's no rest for the weary and no home for the shiftless." I guess she's right.

In the afternoon there was more work to do around the house. Uncle Oliver, once we brought in the mail, retired to Hal Sterling and Outer Space.

"If we're going to keep up the payments on this estate," he said wryly, "I'd better go upstairs to my salt mine and dig." And he did. I think he was glad to have an excuse to escape. Se we pitched in and gave Aunt Claire a hand.

We worked like beavers in a flood. We unpacked things and stashed them away. We held pictures up against the walls while Aunt Claire tried to make up her mind where to hang them. We shoved furniture around. All the time we could hear Charlie Murofino whistling between his teeth as he stroked paint onto the walls.

Obie said to me at one point, "Do you think he'll

remember? About showing us the honey house, I mean."

I shrugged. All the same I, too, was hoping Charlie wouldn't forget.

And then, true to his given word, when Charlie knocked off for the day, he called out, "Come on, if you're coming."

We were after him like a shot.

He led us down the lane and through the highest stand of scraggly locust trees. For once, DeeDee didn't tag along. But the dogs went with us, although Maggie still kept carefully out of our reach.

Halfway there, Maggie suddenly dashed toward one of the trees. Sieglinde dashed at it from the other side. It was a minute before we saw what they were after. They both stood there at the base of the tree, their muzzles pointing up toward the branches. Sieglinde yipped hysterically.

"Look!" Amanda cried. "A squirrel!"

She gazed raptly overhead where the gray creature flicked its fat tail and returned her gaze with a bright beady-eyed stare. It chattered cheekily at us, then leaped to another tree, leaving Maggie and Sieglinde still sniffing around the first trunk. They looked faintly foolish, and I think they knew it.

Obie said, "Really, Amanda. Somebody might think you'd never laid eyes on a squirrel before."

"I've seen lots, in Central Park."

"Well, Central Park doesn't have a monopoly on squirrels," he told her with scorn.

Amanda's eyes shone fiercely. "But these are *our* squirrels!" she cried passionately. Amanda is apt to overdo things a bit. But this time I understood what was going through her mind. What happened then, with that squirrel, was that for the first time she understood what being there at Walkaway Hill was going to mean to her, and, for that matter, to all of us. That was the exact moment when Amanda really fell in love, completely and for all time, with the place. The rest had just been leading up to it. That fat cheeky squirrel, oddly enough, was what clinched the whole thing.

I caught a flicker of amusement in Charlie Murofino's eyes, and he grinned in that quiet way of his. I think that he must have understood too. But the only thing he said was "Look out for the brambles. Those briars can really rip."

Amanda stared out at us solemnly from under that dark thatch of hair.

"Goodness! Well, that's always been the trouble with me," she said with gravity. "I'm always looking at something else and then I end up in a bramble patch."

We all laughed. After a puzzled moment, Amanda joined in.

The brambles were vicious. The narrow path was overgrown with them and we had to advance carefully. Even so, they tore savagely at our clothes. I noticed, too, as we went, that the wind was considerably stronger now. The sky had a curious heaviness. It was like a sheet of lead. But we were too excited about the honey house to pay any attention to that.

Then, suddenly, the honey house was right in front of us.

As I mentioned earlier, it wasn't so much a house as a shack. The windows were grimy and cobwebbed and the walls were sheeted over with old tar paper. Still, it looked sturdy enough.

Charlie was pointing at what looked like a lot of large wooden boxes, painted white and set on the ground all around the shack.

"Those are the hives," he said.

I asked, a little nervously, "Are the bees inside?"

He shook his head.

"No bees left," he said.

"Did the queen fly away somewhere else and take all her subjects with her?" Amanda wanted to know.

He shook his head again.

"They're all dead," he said.

"Oh dear," said Amanda with a sigh.

"Barney Rudkin didn't like the way they buzzed," Charlie went on. "I guess he must of gotten stung once or twice, too, because I came up here one day and I saw where he'd taken a bunch of old rags. Then he'd soaked them in kerosene and stuffed them right where the bees go in and out, and put a match to them. It took care of the bees all right. Smoked them to death. There wasn't any buzzing to upset Barney after that."

After a shocked silence Amanda said, "I think that was a perfectly terrible thing to do."

"It just shows you what you've got to deal with when somebody like Barney Rudkin's around," Charlie said. He spat through his teeth. "And over there is something else that'll show you the kind of person Barney Rudkin is."

We looked where he pointed. The ground all around the honey house was strewn with empty tobacco cans, old soda bottles, discarded baked-bean tins, rusty batteries, and stuff like that. Charlie suddenly stooped, picked something up and examined it. There was a brief flash of gold in his hands. Then he shrugged and tossed it away into the brambles.

"What was that, Charlie?" Obie wanted to know.

"Piece of an old plate."

"Was that all?" Obie sounded disappointed.

"That was enough. I recognized the pattern. It was from Mrs. Houghton's best set. She was kind of proud of those dishes, hardly ever used them, except for something special, and then she always washed them herself. Said they came from someplace in France. I guess they weren't any too good for Barney to use, though." He spat again. "Now that we're here we might as well poke our noses into the shack."

The door of the honey house was open, swinging on its hinges. We followed him in and peered around. It must have been pretty snug once, although right then it looked as though a hurricane had run smack through it. Empty cans and rusty tools were tossed all over the floor and the walls were coated with streaks of thick greasy soot. It smelled kind of nasty, too, like kerosene and worse.

Charlie scratched his head.

"That's funny," he said.

"What's funny?" we demanded.

"There used to be a bed and a dresser and some chairs and a little cook stove in here."

"Maybe the Estate carted it all away," I suggested.

"Not from the looks of things," Charlie said.

"Oh," I said.

"I wonder where all that stuff went to," Charlie muttered, not to anyone in particular, but just sort of thinking out loud. He kicked idly at a pile of junk. Then he said, "Hey!" and bent to examine the heap closely.

"What did you find?" Obie called eagerly. "Something good?"

"Nope," said Charlie. He held something out in his paint-spattered fingers. "Just this."

Amanda said, "It doesn't look like anything at all to me."

Obie said, "Why, it's only a queer-shaped hunk of plaster. It must have come off something."

Charlie turned it over in his hands, and all of a sudden I could tell that it had formed part of an animal, as though it was a piece broken off a model of a dog, or something.

"That was some of her work," Charlie said. "I'd know it anywhere. It's off one of those little statues she used to make."

Amanda said excitedly, "Maybe if we poked around we could find the rest."

"Probably. But what good would that do you?"

"We could glue it all together again, couldn't we? Then we could see what it was. It would be like doing a jigsaw puzzle, only better, because it wouldn't be just flat."

"Maybe. Maybe not." He kicked at the rubbish heap again. "There are the other pieces," he said, "but they're smashed too small. You couldn't do anything with them now."

"Like Humpty Dumpty," observed Amanda ruefully.

Charlie tossed the bit of plaster of paris into a corner.

"Let's get out of here," he said. "I don't like the stink of Barney Rudkin."

After we filed out of the honey house, he carefully closed the door behind us, making sure that it held.

"All the same," he muttered thoughtfully, "I wonder what those pieces of Mrs, Houghton's statue were doing in Barney Rudkin's shack. I can see him using her dishes. But what would he want with that statue? He never was much to care about art, if you know what I mean. And the way it was broken, too: not just in any ordinary way, but as though somebody'd taken a hammer to it and done a pretty thorough job."

I couldn't help gloating at the prospect of a real mystery after all, but I tried not to show it.

"Do you smell a rat, Charlie?" I asked.

He gave me an odd glance.

"More like a skunk, for my money," he said dryly.

We just looked blankly at him, not knowing what to think. I mean, it wasn't as though we'd known Barney Rudkin, or anything like that, so it didn't seem any odder to us than anything else about the honey house.

"Unless," Charlie said, rubbing his chin reflectively, "somebody's been rooting around looking for the money."

"The money?" we all said in a single breath.

Charlie shrugged. "It's only the way they talk in the village. Mrs. Houghton always paid cash for everything, always had plenty of it, and there's always been this story that she had a heap of it stashed on the place." He paused. "Nobody ever found a scrap of it, though, not even those lawyers." He paused again. "Still, there are those who still swear there must be thousands of dollars hidden someplace here. Not that I pay any mind to that sort of scuttlebutt."

Obie said airily, "Oh, piffle. It's only something that could happen in a book. It's the sort of thing Poppa's always using for a plot when he gets stuck."

Amanda had a faraway look. "I'll bet it is true, though. Wouldn't it be wonderful if something did happen to us that was like the things that happen in books! Supposing we found the treasure: we could call the place Treasure Hill!" She broke off, too overwhelmed by the thought to go on.

Personally, although I agreed with Charlie and Obie that it was all a lot of nonsense, I couldn't help thinking that it would be exciting if it did turn out to be true, after all. I mean, I always keep hoping that life will turn out to be like books, although I know it won't.

Charlie said abruptly, "Well, that's that. I'll see you next week." He shook hands with me. "It was nice meeting you, James. Maybe I'll run into you next time you come up this way. So long, all." And he was off, moving through the brambles with that lanky easy stride of his.

"I think he's a pretty nice guy," Obie remarked as we watched him go. Coming from Obie, that was about as big a compliment as you could hope for. We all agreed with him too.

Then, since we were already halfway there, we decided to explore the barn. There was still a faint wash of daylight left.

Maggie, still cautious, went with us, and Sieglinde pattered at her flank. The minute we got to the barn, however, a peculiar thing happened. Maggie just stood in front of it and bared her teeth and growled.

"What do you think is the matter with her now?" Amanda wondered.

Obie was too busy getting that enormous barn door open to attend to anything else. "It's just the usual thing," he snorted. "She's just being crazy Maggie."

Amanda, who knows practically all of Gilbert and Sullivan by heart, began singing:

> "'Daft Madge! Crazy Meg!
> Mad Margaret! Poor Peg!
> He! he! he! he! he!'"

Crazy or not, Maggie kept right on. Her hackles rose. She backed away as the door swung out, and her barking got positively furious. Then, to make matters worse,

Sieglinde joined in. It was something, having to listen to the two of them.

Obie remarked in disgust, "And now Sieglinde's going to end up as cuckoo as Maggie. Don't pay any attention to them. Come on, let's explore this place."

The barn was dim and vast. I accidentally kicked over what must have been an empty pail or something like that, and the sudden noise made my bones tingle. I couldn't help feeling shaky. The dogs got even more excited then, and what with their howling, and the dark, and the yawning space all around, and the musty smell of everything, I felt definitely uncomfortable, which is putting it mildly. I'm generally as brave as the next person, but this was out of the usual run of things. I can't really explain how I felt, but I knew we were in the presence of something—well, if not exactly unearthly, at least it was pretty sinister. I mean, it wasn't just any old barn that could have made me feel that way.

For a moment everything was quiet again. We stood there ready to go forward. At the same time each of us seemed to be waiting for someone else to take the first step.

Something behind us creaked in a slow, drawn-out way.

I jumped.

Then I realized that it was only the barn door swinging back with the wind. I was sort of glad that it was too dark for either of the others to have seen me.

Then Obie said impatiently, "What's the matter with you two anyway?"

I didn't trust myself to say anything.

I heard Amanda gulp. "Nothing's the matter," she said, sort of faintly. "It's just that it's so dark."

"For gosh sakes, who's so afraid of the dark?" Obie said

it so confidently that I couldn't help feeling a little bit ashamed. After all, I told myself, it was only a barn.

A shaft of gray light from the open door streaked across the vast space. Even so, we couldn't make out much. Everything was murky and shadowy and vague. Amanda and I stuck close to Obie.

The deliberate creaking sound came again, followed by an abrupt bang. And then we stood there in absolute darkness.

"What's happened now?" Amanda called out edgily.

"It's only the wind," Obie replied. "It swung that door shut. Who has matches?"

None of us did.

"Anyway," I said, "I've always heard that you're not supposed to light matches in a barn."

"How can we explore if we can't see anything?"

"If we ate carrots all the time, like Mamma says," Amanda remarked, "we could see in the dark."

Obie said contemptuously, "I suppose cats eat carrots. If Mamma wants us to see in the dark she ought to give us fried mice on toast every day for breakfast."

I said, "Listen you two. This is no time to start wrangling. I can't even see my hand in front of my face."

"So what?" Obie snapped. "I'm sure you've seen it before."

I was sure that even Obie was beginning to get nervous by this time, because he only gets sarcastic when he isn't feeling particularly sure of himself.

Then we heard it.

I wasn't sure what it was. I only knew that it was the eeriest sound that I'd ever heard. And we could hear something rustling somewhere up there in the space above our head.

Suddenly I was really scared. I couldn't help it or do

anything about it. I could feel goose pimples rising all over me.

And then, on top of that, Maggie threw her head back and really howled.

Darkness or no darkness, it didn't take us long to stumble to the door, fumble it open, and get outside. When the fresh air finally hit our faces, we were all pretty short of breath.

Dimly, through the trees, we could see the lights of the house. They were the most reassuring thing I'd ever seen. But the sky was very black by now, the wind whistled as though it had gone crazy, and the boughs of the trees whooshed like anything.

Amanda said in a low, unsteady voice, "What do you think it was, exactly, that we heard in there?"

"Probably nothing more than a little old barn owl," Obie replied jauntily. "What do you think, James?"

"Probably," I said, trying to sound nonchalant.

All the same, whatever it was, I was glad that we were out of there.

Obie gave me a queer look. I didn't say anything more, though. I mean, if he wanted to think it was only an owl, that was all right with me. For my part, I was positive that it had been something else, even though I wasn't sure what.

Then all three of us started running, the dogs at our heels. We didn't stop until we got to the house.

8

WHITE STUFF

That night, sometime after supper, it started.

We kept running to the windows to see it. The fat white flurrying flakes came steadily down. It wasn't long before the lane and the lawn and all the fields around the house were settled with white. The trees looked strange and kind of wonderful, as though they were floating. And the wind howled.

Amanda was delirious. "Do you think we'll be snowbound?" she cried. "That would really be something, just like in Longfellow."

"Whittier, I believe it was," Uncle Oliver corrected dryly. Amanda flushed, but not for more than an instant. "Anyway," Uncle Oliver added, "I hope not. We've enough on our hands as it is. And James has to be home by tomorrow night."

"I wouldn't mind missing school," I said, maybe a little too enthusiastically. Obie and I looked at each other.

Then we pressed our noses hopefully against the cold windowpanes, wishing it would really happen.

But Aunt Claire frowned in a worried way.

"Do you think we could actually be snowed in, Oliver?"

He grinned confidently.

"That sort of thing doesn't happen anymore. We've come a long way since Whittier's day."

"All the same," Aunt Claire remarked, sort of to herself, "I'm glad I did all that shopping in the village yesterday morning. There's enough in the icebox to last us a week!"

"If you're really concerned, Claire, we could turn on the radio and absorb the weather reports."

"It wouldn't change it, even if we did listen, would it?"

Uncle Oliver gave her one of those understanding glances that they're forever exchanging. "I guess not," he said. He had lit a fire in the living room, and now the logs snapped and popped while the white stuff whirled outside. Sieglinde lay with her backside hugging the fire screen, sighing windily. And just then Mrs. MacMinnies appeared from the kitchen with a pot of cocoa and a load of sugar cookies. We all felt pretty snug and cheerful—that is, until we suddenly thought of Maggie out there in the storm. We peered through the misting glass. Sure enough, there she was, her muzzle grizzled with snowflakes, barking like anything as she streaked through the drifts.

"She looks like a wolf," Obie said.

"A werewolf," I put in, shivering a little.

"She looks positively spooky," Amanda said. "I wish we could get her to come inside. I'm sure she'd love it by the fire, once she came in."

Well, we went to the front door and called and called.

But for all the attention that crazy collie paid us, we were the ones who might have been the ghosts. So we gave up, finally. We had to. Uncle Oliver was shouting about the cold air we were letting into the house, and the price of heating fuel.

Aunt Claire stitched away on a pile of curtains, and Mrs. MacMinnies had her glasses on, which meant she was in for a session of darning. Uncle Oliver blinked benignly through his spectacles and rubbed his hands. "Well," he said, "now that everything looks so cheerful in here, what shall we do? Anyone for a giddy game of Scrabble, or a hysterical session of In the Manner of the Adverb?"

"We can't start games now," Aunt Claire said. "It's practically bedtime."

"It's Saturday night," Amanda pleaded. "After all—"

"Let them stay up a little while longer, Claire," Uncle Oliver said. "The fire's still going strong. We might as well enjoy it while it lasts. Besides, we can't go upstairs until it's out."

"Well," Aunt Claire said, weakening.

"I want to hear stories," DeeDee commanded.

Uncle Oliver looked around. For once, an idea of DeeDee's met with unanimous approval from the rest of us. He rose. "Let's see," he said. "What'll it be? There's de la Mare, and Saki. I remember unpacking both of them."

"Couldn't we tell stories tonight," Amanda said, "instead of just reading them?"

"Hey," said Obie eagerly, "how about ghost stories this time?"

"Obie, really!" Aunt Claire said with a significant glance in DeeDee's direction.

"Don't say 'Obie, really!,' Mamma," DeeDee said. "I *want* to hear about spooks and witches and all."

Mrs. MacMinnies raised her eyes from her darning. "The Lord save us!" she exclaimed. "I had enough of that sort of thing when I was a girl on the other side of the water. My old Gran, may her poor departed soul rest in peace, was forever telling us how she heard the banshees."

Amanda's eyes glowed the way they always do when she hears about something that's mysterious and possibly on the poetic side. "Tell us, Mrs. MacMinnies. Please!"

Mrs. MacMinnies bit off a length of black thread. "Not much to tell," she replied matter-of-factly. "They come and wail under the windows of the house for a night or two, just before somebody dies."

We were all more or less impressed.

"But what are they?"

Mrs. MacMinnies shrugged her bony shoulders. "The dear knows. Some say they're spirits, all gotten up to look like beautiful ladies, and they keen and comb their hair all the while. And it's always to some member of the family of the one who's about to die that they appear."

Amanda's eyes got positively saucerish.

"Did you ever see them or hear them, Mrs. MacMinnies?"

Mrs. MacMinnies regarded Amanda in astonishment.

"I?" she said. "Certainly not. They didn't have them anymore when I was a girl. Anyway, not in Liverpool, where I was born."

"But your grandmother—" Obie began.

"My old Gran was raised in Ireland," Mrs. MacMinnies retorted decisively. "Everything was different there. And what's more, she's been gone a long time."

We all fell silent. There was only the crackling of the

logs in the fire, and a sudden shower of sparks. Then the room was very quiet.

"Listen!" Amanda whispered suddenly.

We all listened, uneasily.

Through the stillness we could make out a weird high sound. It was exactly like someone wailing out there in the blizzard, just beyond the windows. I'm not ashamed to admit that it made me shiver. I would have sworn at that moment that it was one of those old Irish banshees, keening in the night to warn us of something dreadful that was about to happen.

Mrs. MacMinnies raised her eyes to the ceiling and hastily crossed herself.

Suddenly Uncle Oliver's laughter bounced across the room.

"For goodness' sake," he said. "It's only Maggie."

"Amanda!" Aunt Claire said, the color coming back into her face. "With your imagination—"

Then we all started to laugh.

"Come to think of it," Uncle Oliver said slowly, "I remember a story I heard when I was a boy. It was about the ghost of a hunting dog. An Irish setter it was," he added, with a smile in Mrs. MacMinnies's direction.

She merely sniffed and went on with her mending.

Amanda and Obie and I flopped on the floor in front of him. "Tell us, Poppa," Amanda said.

"This was up in Maine, where we used to go every summer. There was a local character who'd come along once in a while whenever we boys built a bonfire on the beach. He was a real storyteller, old Dwight, but there was something about the way he told his stories that made you realize he wasn't just making them up. Well, old Dwight was a great one for going after birds. He had a handsome brace of setters. I can remember them still:

Tom and Digger they were called. We all admired them a lot.

"One night, when the bonfire was sinking, Dwight said, 'Yep, I won't deny they're fine dogs. Good noses on the both of them. But they're not a patch on old Josie. Why, Josie saved my life. And the funny thing is, it happened after she was dead.'

"Of course, we had to know how that had happened.

"Old Dwight scratched himself through his faded shirt.

"'Even if I did tell you, you probably wouldn't believe it.'

"Naturally we all promised up and down and sideways that we'd believe his story, no matter what it was.

"And so he told us.

"It seemed that Josie was the finest hunting dog in the township. She had the keenest nose and the most affectionate ways of any setter Dwight had ever raised. They were always together. No matter where old Dwight went, Josie tagged along like his mahogany-colored shadow. Until one day when some crazy fool ran over her. And that was the end of Josie.

"Only it wasn't, really.

"Old Dwight didn't want any other dog after Josie. He didn't even have the heart to go out after birds. He just hung his gun up on the wall over his bed and tried to forget about it.

"One afternoon—he remembered later that it was a year to the day after Josie got killed—he was lying on his bed, trying to nap. But he couldn't shut his eyes. It was a clear autumn day, the leaves had turned, and the birds were pretty plump that year. He kept feeling restless in a funny way. It wasn't the way you feel after too many steamed clams, he explained, but as though there were something out in the woods and marshes beyond the town that was calling him out into the crisp fall weather. Finally he just couldn't stand it any longer. He lifted his gun down from the rack and put on his red lumber jacket and went outside. It seemed to him then that he could hear a dog calling to him from away out there in the middle of the marsh. And it couldn't be any other dog but Josie.

"He thought he was plumb crazy, of course. But all the same, he kept following the sound. Before long he realized that, although he knew those marshes pretty well, he was lost. He couldn't find his way out. Everywhere he turned, the ooze only got deeper. Those marshes were treacherous, too. More than one careless hunter had been pulled out of there, drowned and frozen stiffer than a plank.

"He figured at last that he was a goner.

"But he fancied that he could still hear Josie's unmistakable yelping. He didn't really believe it, but he figured it was worth a try, so he whistled to her in the old way."

"And?" Obie asked in a breathless voice, not wanting to interrupt Uncle Oliver's story, but at the same time unable to keep still.

"And then," Uncle Oliver said, "sure enough, Josie came loping up to him. She ran to his side and licked his hands.

"We asked Dwight if he was certain it was Josie.

"He just nodded solemnly.

"'The skin was a mite loose,' he said, 'but it was Josie, all right.' And then, with Josie leading him, he was able to pick his way out of the marsh to safety. And they went hunting, just as they had in the old days. Dwight ended up with a couple brace of plump partridge. And just as night was falling, Josie led him right up to his gate, and with a wag of her tail she was gone. She just sort of evaporated into the evening."

"And that was the last he ever saw of her?"

"That was the last time old Dwight ever saw Josie."

We stared into the fire, thinking about the story.

Aunt Claire said, very quietly, "You never told me that one before, Oliver."

"I guess I forgot about it. It's years since I last thought of old Dwight and his dog. I suppose it was listening to Maggie yelping out there that made me remember it again."

Mrs. MacMinnies's darning lay idle in her lap.

"I remember a story about a priest." There was a strange expression on her face. "Mind you," she said, "this was one of my Gran's stories. She had what they call 'second sight,' and anything about ghosts and banshees and all that was no more to her than the news in the daily paper." For a minute Mrs. MacMinnies fell silent and looked away. It was as though she wasn't there anymore with the rest of us, but was seeing her grandmother's face instead. Then she abruptly shook her head.

"There was this old priest, Father Scanlon his name was, that my old Gran knew about. I'm not sure, but I think he must have been the parish priest of the village where she was born and that she grew to a girl in. Oh, he was the learned one, Father Scanlon, if you'd believe what my Gran said, what with having the Gaelic and the Latin and the Hebrew and the Greek and all. But one day, in spite of all his books and his holiness, the old man passed on. And it was a grand funeral they gave him, for everyone loved him, since along with everything else, he was a good man.

"Well, after that, they had this young priest come from

Belfast to take over. Poor man, it was bad enough stepping, a stranger to the place, into old Father Scanlon's shoes, but there was worse.

"Every night as the young priest lay in his bed he saw this strange thing. It was like a light, shining like a torch from another world, across the room onto the old man's bookshelves. The young father wasn't afraid—for isn't it the things of the other world that they're taught to look after in the seminary?—but it was a great perplexity to him. He looked at it without a blink to his eye, saying his Hail Marys and the Our Father, but still the thing wouldn't budge. Even after he put the bed light out it kept shining there to his botheration. And this went on night after night. He had all the lamps seen to, but there was nothing wrong with them. He pulled down the shades and drew the curtains, to be sure no one could be shining their torches through the windows. The poor man, he did everything he could think of.

"After a time this got to be a terrible affliction to the young priest, fresh out of the priests' college as he was, and this beyond anything he'd learned from the good fathers there. He was beside himself with trying to figure it out. He even called in the bishop. But it was no use, and the wonder of it spread to all the villages for miles, and priests rained down like crows from Belfast and Dublin and the dear knows where all. And the village was getting a swelled head from all the notice that was being taken of it. But all that made no difference.

"One night when he could snatch no sleep at all from watching that light from nowhere that was sporting about Father Scanlon's books, he got out of his bed, just as he was, in his nightshirt and naked feet and all. And he went through every one of those blessed books, Hebrew and Gaelic and Latin and Greek, page by blessed page. When he came to the very last one he saw that it was the breviary that old Father Scanlon had been reading just before his death fell on him. And there, stuck right between the last page and the cover, was two pound-notes with a letter asking for ten masses for the dead. They must have been given to Father Scanlon, but he'd passed on before those masses could be said.

"Well, the young father lost no time in saying those masses, and after that there was no more light shining on those books."

She paused.

"So you can see, it's like my old Gran used to say, it's not every ghost that comes back to do harm. There's those that come back with kindness, to make sure their work is properly finished, so that those poor departed souls can rest in peace, please God."

It was Aunt Claire who broke the silence that followed Mrs. MacMinnies's story. We were all sure that she was going to change the subject and make us talk about something else because DeeDee was there. Little pitchers, and so on and so forth. But instead, she simply said, "I know a story about a friendly ghost. It's supposed to be real." She wrinkled her forehead. "Although for the life of me I can't recall where I heard it."

"Let's have it, Claire," Uncle Oliver said.

"As you know," Aunt Claire said, "I'm not much at telling stories." She smiled. "I'm not a writer and I'm not Irish. But I'll do my best. It's a story about a haunted farmhouse."

We all shuddered a little with expectation and drew closer along the floor to her chair.

"As you know, most haunted houses have ghosts who rattle chains or pull the blankets off people while they're sleeping, or send china flying through the air."

Amanda nodded excitedly. "Like in *Wuthering Heights*," she exclaimed, "when Cathy—"

Obie silenced her with a nudge of his elbow.

"This isn't about a ghost like that," Aunt Claire went on. "This is about a man who had a farm that he loved very much. I can't even remember his name. Let's say he was Mr. Brown."

"Not a very original name, dear," Uncle Oliver observed critically.

Aunt Claire pursed her lips. Uncle Oliver squinched down apologetically in his seat and let her continue.

"Mr. Brown worked like a slave day and night to make his farm the nicest one for miles around. He worked so hard doing the milking and caring for the garden and everything that he caught pneumonia. On his deathbed he told his wife never to sell the place out of the family. He had planned it for his children to have after him. 'If you do sell this farm,' he said, 'I'll come back and haunt whoever buys it.' And those were the very last words he said.

"After that his wife did her best to keep up the place, but it wasn't easy. The children were still too small to be much help, and she couldn't afford a hired man, so she simply had to sell it. A young couple who had just been married were eager to buy it, and finally she agreed to let them.

"For a moment, as she signed the papers that turned the place over to the young couple, she remembered her dead husband's last words. She couldn't help shivering a little, but of course she didn't really believe in ghosts and hauntings, and even if she did, it was already too late to do anything about it. So she didn't mention it, and she took the money and packed everything and left the farm and moved away to the city with her children.

"Things went well enough with the new couple for a while. The young man was a hard worker and he really loved the farm. Soon everything was back to the way it had been when Mr. Brown was alive. Then the couple had a baby: a fine pudgy little boy.

"The day the husband brought his wife home with their new baby, she was alone in the kitchen, feeding it, when a face appeared at the window.

"She was a sensible woman, so she wasn't startled or anything. The face smiled reassuringly at her, so she smiled too. And then the face was gone.

"When her husband came in from the barn, she said: 'Who was that at the window, dear? He looked like such a nice man.' Her husband looked at her oddly. 'There's been no one about on the place,' he told her, 'not even a tramp. You're tired. You'd better go upstairs and lie down.' But she insisted that she had seen someone.

"The next day, at the same time, when she was nursing her baby, the face appeared again, smiling again, and it was such an open, friendly smile that she didn't call out for her husband. She simply smiled back. And then he made a sort of sign to her. At first she didn't understand what he wanted, but he kept on making that beckoning sign, until eventually she realized that he wanted to see the baby. She held the baby up for him to admire and he seemed satisfied. He smiled again, nodded, and went away. And she never again saw that face at the window.

"About a week later, however, something very peculiar did happen.

"The young couple had decided that, what with the new baby, and the farm going so well, and everything, it was time to have a party on the day of the baby's christening. All the relatives from both sides of the family were invited, and a lot of the neighbors too. And when they all came back from the church there was a big picnic on the front lawn. Everyone had a marvelous time, eating and gossiping and playing games; and just before it broke up they all stood in a group in front of the house while a photographer took a picture. When the photograph was developed, there, in one of the parlor windows, was a man's smiling face. It was the same man who had appeared to the young wife. And the neighbors recognized him at once."

"It was Mr. Brown!" Amanda cried.

Aunt Claire nodded.

By this time our eyes were bugging out of our faces. We were full of speculation, and we could have gone right on until morning listening to stories of ghosts and hauntings. But the fire was dying, and Uncle Oliver looked at his watch.

"All right," he said. "Bed."

We knew there was no putting off the evil moment this time.

Amanda and Obie and DeeDee and I got up from the floor and stretched. My leg tingled. It had gone to sleep.

Amanda ran to the window.

"It's still snowing," she announced, "more than ever. And there's Maggie, still rushing around in it. Poor thing, it's a shame."

Mrs. MacMinnies didn't say anything. She just strode out to the kitchen while we tagged, curious, after her, thinking there might be more cookies in the offing.

Mrs. MacMinnies's mind, however, was not on cookies.

She flung open the porch door, and we could feel the wild wind whip around the door.

Mrs. MacMinnies stood there with her hands on her hips.

She said in a clear sharp voice, "Maggie."

Maggie stopped running.

Mrs. MacMinnies said, "Come into the house now, you crazy creature."

Maggie remained motionless in her tracks. The snow was already up to her chest. She looked up uncertainly at Mrs. MacMinnies. She could just as well have been a snow dog: her coat and everything else was white, except for her eyes. They looked like two burning coals, the way they reflected the light from the porch.

"Did you hear me, Maggie?" Mrs. MacMinnies said firmly. "I can't stand here freezing all the blessed night. Make up your mind, now. In or out."

And then to our unending astonishment, Maggie floundered toward the house, lumbered up the steps of the porch, and scuttled through the door. She made a beeline for the hall. For a few seconds she stood there nervously. Then she turned around a few times and at last flumped down on the little round rug that had WELCOME woven into it.

Mrs. MacMinnies closed the kitchen door and bolted it.

"That's more like," she declared briskly as we all gaped at her. She turned on us. "And now," she said, "you'd best go up to bed and leave her be until she gets used to it. Now that she's safely inside there's no sense fussing her."

Amanda gasped. "But how did you ever—"

"Never you mind," Mrs. MacMinnies told her sternly. "Up to your rooms, now, the lot of you."

We all began trailing upstairs, taking care to circle Maggie by a wide margin. She did look pretty wild and bedraggled lying there in the freshly painted hall, the snow melting off her rough coat in trickles. She hadn't even shaken herself off.

We could hear Mrs. MacMinnies telling Aunt Claire not to worry about the wet: she'd take care of it herself in the morning.

We had reached the top of the stairs when DeeDee suddenly remembered Sieglinde. Sieglinde always slept on an old car blanket at the foot of DeeDee's bed.

"Sieglinde!" she called.

But there was no answering patter of Sieglinde's paws.

"Sieglinde!" DeeDee called again, more shrilly. "You come right upstairs to bed!"

It was as though Sieglinde had not heard at all.

DeeDee stamped her foot.

And still there was no sign of Sieglinde.

We crouched at the head of the stairs and peered down. Sieglinde had curled herself into a ball at Maggie's side. She didn't even blink up at DeeDee. Nothing would budge her.

And that was that.

DeeDee was pretty stubborn, but Sieglinde was even more so.

Finally, with Aunt Claire's help, we got DeeDee calmed down. After that none of us wasted too much time saying good night and brushing our teeth and getting undressed.

I dashed into my room. It was cold. I jumped into bed. My teeth were rattling. The snow spun against the windowpane, crusting it thickly, so that I could barely see out. The branches, heavy with snow, pecked against the glass, as though they were relaying some eerie message in Morse code. I clutched the blankets tightly around me. I didn't want any ghosts whipping them off me while I slept.

9

THE ABOMINABLE SNOWMAN

I'm not sure what woke me.

I think it was Obie and Amanda galloping through the hall to the bathroom. A minute later there was Obie pounding on my door and yelling something about making the biggest snowman in the world.

I opened my eyes. Then I quickly shut them again. I had to. Then I tried opening them as gradually as I could. The light in the uncurtained room was positively blinding. I mean it really hurt to look. I had to keep rubbing my eyes in order to get used to it. All the same, I couldn't help feeling a kind of crazy excitement.

Everything was white. It was just as if, overnight, Walkaway Hill had been turned into an enormous cake covered with white sugar icing, and the sun was shining over it, making everything sparkle. It was pretty dazzling, even when your eyes got used to it. I got up, clutching the warm blankets around me, and went to the window. Everything as far as I could see was covered with the stuff: trees, outbuildings, the wood-shed roof, the shrubbery, everything. It hardly seemed like the same place. Away off, at the crest of the hill behind the house, I could make out something bright, like little stumpy birthday candles sticking up. It was a minute before I realized that it was the red tips of the sumac, now level with the snow. And the strangest thing about it all was the quietness. You can't imagine how quiet everything was, now that the wind had died down. The silence was like a roar. It was weird, like watching a movie when the sound track is turned off.

You can take my word for it: it was a pretty marvelous thing to wake up at Walkaway Hill that snowy Sunday morning.

I didn't want to miss a moment of it. I threw on my clothes, splashed water on my face, raked my fingers through my hair, and scooted downstairs.

The first living thing I saw was Maggie, hugging that WELCOME rug as though it were a life raft. And Sieglinde was dug into her side like a burdock sticker. Maggie, when she saw me, moved uneasily and made sort of a half growl of nervousness in her throat, but I took care to reassure her by not going too near. I could hear the radio going in the kitchen. Obie and Amanda were already there, fully dressed and their eyes bright with excitement. So was DeeDee, but she looked kind of mopey in spite of the snow and everything. I figured Sieglinde's unfaithfulness had done that to her. Aunt Claire and Uncle Oliver were still upstairs.

Mrs. MacMinnies plunked our breakfast down on the table without a word.

"Is anything wrong, Mrs. MacMinnies?" I asked.

Amanda and Obie were wigwagging signals to me to shut up, but I noticed them too late.

"Wrong?" said Mrs. MacMinnies in a voice from which all cheer had been carefully expunged. It was a voice as cold as the landscape beyond the window. "Wrong? Just listen to that radio if you want to know what's wrong."

I listened. The local weather report was nearly over, but I could still get the tail end of it. ". . . And several inches more are expected before the day is over. According to the latest word we have had, the storm will continue well into the afternoon. Motorists are warned not to venture out. While some of the main roads have been partly cleared, drifting snow has made driving precarious everywhere in this area, especially off the main parkways. Further reports on the weather and road conditions will be broadcast hourly. Keep tuned to this station for the latest developments. And now, folks, it's our pleasure to give you the latest recording by those masters of popular vocalization, the Hot Rod Boys. They will sing for you in their own inimitable style, 'Baby, It's Cold Outside.'"

Mrs. MacMinnies turned it off with a sharp snap.

"That's what's wrong," she said, thin-lipped. "A body can't even get to morning mass on a Sunday from this godforsaken place."

DeeDee said, "Anyway, I'm glad I don't have to go to Sunday school."

Mrs. MacMinnies set the milk bottle down on the table with a bang. She regarded DeeDee steadily. Her face was shocked. "Don't let me hear you talk that way, young lady. If you don't go to Sunday school, how can you expect to get to Heaven afterward?"

DeeDee tossed her angel curls. "But I don't want to go to Heaven."

Mrs. MacMinnies's eyes narrowed in her bony face. "And why not, may I ask?"

"I'd get tired," DeeDee chirped. "All those stairs."

Amanda began to giggle, but a look from Mrs. Mac-Minnies squelched her. DeeDee stuck her tongue out at Amanda and then hastily buried her face in her milk mug before Mrs. MacMinnies could see. I wanted to laugh too, but I didn't dare. The atmosphere was already electric enough. So I turned my face toward the window.

"Holy smoke!" I shouted.

The sun had suddenly clouded over. The sky was dull and gray and heavy. All the brilliance had died out of the morning, and as I watched I could actually see the wind rise, sending snow dervishes whirling over the white crust. And more flakes began to fall. This time they didn't just float down in an airy-fairy way. They pelted.

Mrs. MacMinnies regarded the prospect bleakly. "Well," she said at last, addressing no one in particular, "what can't be cured must be endured. As my Gran used to say, 'If we live through the winter, the Devil wouldn't kill us in summer.'"

We ate our breakfast in silence.

We were just about finished when Uncle Oliver and Aunt Claire came down. Uncle Oliver rubbed his hands together. "What do you think of this?" he said cheerily. "Wonderful weather for walruses!"

That was too much for Mrs. MacMinnies. Wordlessly, but with dignity, she retreated to her own room.

Uncle Oliver mouthed, "What's the matter with her?"

"Church," Obie said. "She can't get to it."

"I'm afraid James can't get home today either," Aunt Claire put in, worriedly. "We were listening to the radio up in our room, and even if we could get the car out of the garage, which we can't, and down the lane, which is impossible, I don't see how we'd ever manage to make it to the station to catch your train, James."

"We couldn't even make it with snow tires," Uncle Oliver declared, "if we had snow tires."

I was quite magnanimous about the whole situation. I said that I didn't really want to inconvenience anyone, and that under the circumstances I would be perfectly happy to stay on indefinitely at Walkaway Hill.

"We'll have to ring up your father and tell him," Aunt Claire continued, doing her best to appear auntish and responsible. She glanced up at the kitchen clock. "Do you think it's too early to call him now? After all, it is Sunday morning."

"He won't mind," I assured her. "He's usually awake at this hour. He likes to get a head start on the Sunday crossword puzzle."

So we called up the Old Man.

I talked to him first. He sounded pretty cheerful. When I told him about the weather, he said, "Well, it's snowing a little here too. But there are plenty of taxis cruising around. You ought to be able to get home, one way or another."

I told him I'd let him talk to Aunt Claire.

"The snow is really quite heavy here, Jim," she said. "And our lane is nearly half a mile long. You can't even see a trace of it now. We don't even know if we'll get plowed out by tonight."

"Oh," the Old Man said. "I guess that means that James will have to miss a day of school."

I tried to look properly doleful about that.

"Just send him along as soon as you can tomorrow,

then, will you, Claire? I think I might get around to missing him by then," the Old Man said.

"I don't think you really understand, Jim," Aunt Claire replied. "I think perhaps I'd better let Oliver talk to you."

Uncle Oliver took possession of the receiver.

"Look here, Jim, I want you to understand that we're in the country," he said. "What? . . . I said, in the country." His voice rose. "Can you hear me? . . . Oh . . . Well, I am shouting, and the point is that we can't be sure how long this thing is going to last . . . I said, the way things are, there's no telling how long we'll be holed in here . . . What? . . . No, I don't want you to send the Canadian Mounties. . . . Listen. We'll ship James home as soon as we can get out . . . You'll have to speak up, old man. The wind's getting stronger. . . . What? . . . I can't hear you. . . . I said I couldn't hear you, Jim." His face went blank. He turned to Aunt Claire. "I think he hung up."

"That's not like Jim. Here, let me try talking to him again."

She took the receiver and listened.

"I guess he did hang up, after all," she said. "There isn't even a buzz now. Or do you think you got cut off by mistake?" She clicked a few times. "Operator? Operator! Oh dear, I wish telephones would behave properly sometimes. One is always getting disconnected just when one doesn't want to be."

Obie said quietly, "May I try it for a second?"

"I suppose it wouldn't do any harm. Anyway, you're the mechanical one in this family."

Obie took it from her and listened intently. Then he spun the dial a few times. After that he nodded and set the thing back on its cradle.

Uncle Oliver, lifting his eyebrows, said, "Well, young Alexander Graham Bell, what's the verdict?"

"It's dead," Obie announced.

"Dead?" Aunt Claire cried. "Oh, no!"

"On the blink. Out of commission." Obie waved at the outdoors. "Perhaps you've noticed there's a storm going on outside. It must have knocked down a pole or something."

Aunt Claire looked at her husband wildly. "Oliver, they'll have to come and fix it at once. Supposing one of the children were to get sick, or—"

"Now, Claire," Uncle Oliver said, "take it easy. How can we let them know? And how would they get here in all this?"

"Oh dear," Aunt Claire said. Suddenly it all seemed to sink in. "Then we're really snowbound. We're helpless. I mean—" She stared in dismay at Uncle Oliver, then at us. "Well, that means we're cut off from absolutely everything, doesn't it?"

We did our best not to look too exultant.

"I guess it does," said Obie.

Obie and Amanda and I spent the rest of that morning trying to read, but none of the books we could lay our hands on managed to hold our interest. We kept looking up from the dull dead pages to see what the wild weather was doing. The snow was dumping down from the sky and bucketing through the heavy air so that there was no question of our getting permission to go outside. Mrs. MacMinnies had returned to the kitchen, where she was grimly putting together Sunday dinner. Aunt Claire and Uncle Oliver were no fun either. Uncle Oliver was in his study with Hal Sterling. Aunt Claire was somewhere upstairs. And that, for the time being, was the end of them. Maggie still kept to her rug. She was very quiet, but whenever anyone approached she still sort of cringed in that nervous way of hers and let out an involuntary growl. As for Sieglinde, nothing could pry her from Maggie's side.

In fact, the only diversion we could scare up was trying to get a rise out of DeeDee by telling her how, when the snow in the country got really high, like now, bears and mountain lions and wolves would sneak down from their lairs to prowl around lonely houses, looking for food.

DeeDee refused to be intimidated.

"I'd just sick Sieglinde on them," she declared.

"They'd gobble Sieglinde up in a trice," Obie told her. "Why, that fat dachshund would only be a mouthful to them."

"I'd just like to see them try," DeeDee said stolidly.

"But Sieglinde wouldn't stand a chance," Amanda insisted. "It would just be life in the raw, nature red in tooth and claw." I could see Amanda's imagination take hold, sweeping her along. "They'd be ravenous, starving, growling, their guts all rumbling and their jaws slavering and their fangs bare and their ribs sticking out from hunger. They'd come creeping, creeping, creeping, creeping. And then they'd pounce."

DeeDee stared at Amanda for a full minute. Then her eyes grew very wide and her lower lip began to quiver.

"I'm going to tell Poppa," she said.

So we had to reassure her and calm her down again. But every so often she'd peer suspiciously at us from under her lashes, and we'd have to start reassuring her all over again. After a while we were thoroughly sorry we'd ever started. A little teasing can be fun now and again when you've got the right person for a goat. You have to think twice, though, before you try anything like that with DeeDee.

Just when we were so bored with goofing around with DeeDee and having to stay indoors that we were all ready to pick on each other, the wind abruptly died down: just like that. The snow stopped falling. The sun came out and everything sparkled again, as though powdered with precious stones. Obie sprinted upstairs and came back pronto with Uncle Oliver's permission to go outside.

It didn't take more than a minute for us to get bundled up and out into that snow. The instant the front door was opened, Maggie shot out through it, like a cork from a bottle, and Sieglinde pursued her like a loving bullet.

We stood huddled on the porch and watched them. It was really pretty funny to see them floundering and sniffing through the high drifts, their muzzles and eyebrows caterpillared with white. Sieglinde went crazy with it. She would dive right in, bounding up again to look over toward Maggie. Then she would dash under the surface again, so that only her spiky tail showed, sticking straight up like a rusty nail.

And then we went after them, plunging off the drifted front porch into all the wonderful white stuff.

Obie whooped and hollered. Amanda emitted a sigh of poetic ecstasy. DeeDee screeched and held on to Amanda. But I didn't do any of those things.

I just stood still, blinking, for a couple of seconds.

I didn't want to do anything but just be there, right in the middle of it, and drink it all in. I wanted to look at it and feel it and taste it and *know* it. Because I'd never seen snow like that in my life before. I mean real snow, not the tame and dirty city slush that they shovel off the streets and load into Sanitation Department dump trucks. I don't know if I can explain this exactly, but it was as though I was there all alone with that wonderful whiteness all around me. I wanted to shut out the voices of the others. I felt like the first man on the moon and I didn't want it spoiled by anyone's talking or making a sound, or anything. It was like being in the middle of the sky or the middle of the sea or lost in the uncharted wastes of the desert. There wasn't a track that you could see, or even the faintest sign of where the lane had been. The outbuildings were blanketed out of sight. The trees hung heavy with the stuff and the mountains beyond Walkaway Hill were like enormous white clouds, and it all stretched everywhere without any beginning and without any end to it so far as I could tell. It was—well, it was just there, and I was there too. Then Obie made a grab for me and I went right down into it.

After that there was no holding us. We staggered around in that snow like wild Indians or crazy Eskimos or something. We didn't even stop to pack snowballs. We just threw great powdery armfuls of it into each other's faces, laughing all the time, and wading through it up to our hips and stumbling and picking ourselves up and starting all over again. We could feel it melt down under our collars and come trickling in over the tops of our galoshes.

It was all absolutely glorious.

And then Uncle Oliver in his overcoat and mittens, with a scarf shrouding his chin, appeared on the front porch.

"I finally ran these down to earth in the cellar," he called out, laughing, as he tossed two shovels and an old broom into the snow.

Well, we shoveled and we swept, but we really couldn't manage to make much of a path, it was so deep, and the snow was surprisingly heavy once we tried moving it. So we figured that it would be enough to clear off the porches and make a sort of trench connecting them. When that was finished we cleared a space beside the trench, a space big enough to hold a snowman.

That snowman, when we started it, wasn't anything out of the ordinary. But it kept getting bigger all the time. Before we realized it we had a giant out there in front of the house. We rooted around under the snow and found stones for the buttons. Obie dashed into the house and came out again with an old mop, which he spread out on top of the head. It looked like scraggly gray witch hair. Then he put a bucket on top of that, and I stuck a broomstick into the part that looked like the crook of the arm. Amanda carved features of a sort, which succeeded in making that snowman seem even more ogreish, and DeeDee amused herself by putting little snowballs all around the middle part, giving him what she insisted was a polka-dotted vest.

When we had done everything to it that we could possibly think of, we backed up and surveyed our creation.

"It's horrendous!" Obie crowed.

"What a creep!" Amanda called out, shuddering happily.

"Now we have to name it," DeeDee piped.

I suggested the Colossus of Walkaway Hill.

"Not bad," admitted Obie.

Amanda was squinting at it. "But it's—it's the Abominable Snowman!"

And so the Abominable Snowman it was, except that DeeDee kept calling it the Abdominable Snowman. We linked hands and did a victory dance around it, whooping like Mohicans with a paleface prisoner. Maggie and

Sieglinde stopped snuffling in the snowbanks, looked startled, and then raced around us, barking excitedly. It was as though they had decided to join in our fun.

We danced and whooped until we were exhausted and out of breath. We flopped onto our backs in the snow and lay there gasping, pooped to a frazzle, with the Abominable Snowman casting its grotesque shadow over us. Amanda giggled quietly to herself and Obie and I flung our arms over our eyes because the sun was so bright as to be practically unbearable. We could hear the dogs panting. I don't think any one of us paid any attention to what DeeDee was doing.

For a while everything was marvelously still. I watched the color that shifted and changed like the bits in one of those glass tubes, behind my closed eyelids. It was kind of amusing to think that I was being a human kaleidoscope.

It was DeeDee who broke the silence.

"I touched her!" we heard her cry. "I touched her!"

We jerked to sitting positions. There was DeeDee crouched beside Maggie, her mittens off and her pudgy fingers resting on the collie's mane. Her face was suffused with a look of terrible joy and pride.

"Maggie let me touch her!" DeeDee said it in a hushed triumphant voice. The rest of us stared at her in wonder and envy. I might add that Obie and Amanda and I shared a certain bitterness at the thought that, of all of us, it was the detestable DeeDee to whom Maggie had give the first sign of trust.

And then, evidently afraid that she had advanced too far, Maggie became cautious again, turned tail and retreated, tunneling through the snow with Sieglinde after her.

Fortunately, DeeDee didn't have time to gloat over her

victory, because Mrs. MacMinnies was rapping on the windowpane to call us in to dinner. It was a specially fine Sunday dinner, too: one of Mrs. MacMinnies's best. She had presumably gotten over not being able to go to church, since she produced chicken and dumplings and cranberry sauce and fresh cornbread and pistachio ice cream and a really knockout coconut triple-layer cake. I'm mentioning this not because I'm greedier than anybody else but because I think it's only fair to give credit where credit is due.

After dinner we just sat around. There was nothing else to do. I think it was chiefly the dumplings that made us so logy, although two helpings of cake might have had some share in it. Then we helped with the dishes. Then we all bundled up again and went outside because Aunt Claire and Uncle Oliver and Mrs. MacMinnies had to admire the snowman from close up.

It wasn't snowing anymore, but the wind was high again, making drifts all over the parts we'd cleared. The Abominable Snowman, however, still stood there unmarred. If anything, he looked even solider than before. He was pretty terrific, if I do say so myself, especially because by then the sun had begun to set. I ought to explain that I'm not much on sunsets myself, particularly when there are people around who feel they have to exclaim over them, like Amanda. But there was no denying that the deep red glow on all that snow was nothing short of sensational.

The dogs came closer to us now, although Maggie seemed to have repented of her earlier indiscretion with DeeDee. What was interesting was how their coats shone after all that fooling around in the snow. I mean, it looked as though they'd been to the dry cleaners. Maggie didn't look half the disgrace she'd been when I first laid eyes on her.

"I'd certainly like to take a currycomb to her now," Mrs. MacMinnies said with a glint in her eye.

Then, suddenly, the sunset was over. Darkness fell like a cannonball.

We went inside.

Amanda and I were in the hall, still struggling with our galoshes, when we got the first inkling that something was wrong.

We could hear Uncle Oliver using what Aunt Claire calls "language." Then we heard Aunt Claire remonstrating. After that his voice came loud and clear: "How in blazes can I help barking my shins on all this stuff if you won't switch on the lights?"

"But I did snap the switch, Oliver, and nothing happened. I suppose the bulb is burned out."

"Then try another. What about the bridge lamp?"

"I can't find it. Oh, here it is." There was a pause. "I think that bulb's gone, too."

"Drat. Where's Obie?"

"I'm right here," Obie said. We heard a number of clicks, and then Obie's calm voice. "I think one of the fuses must have blown, Poppa."

"Oh," said Uncle Oliver. "I suppose that means I've got to crawl down into that dark cellar and fix it."

At the same instant Mrs. MacMinnies's voice from the kitchen proclaimed that none of the blessed lights were working. The next moment DeeDee piped in a tone of personal grievance, "I can't see anything!"

By then I'd managed to yank off my galoshes. The shoes were still inside. By the time I had wrenched the shoes out and put them on, Obie had found a flashlight and a carton of electric fuses.

The three of us trekked down to the cellar to fix the lights.

We tried every fuse there was. The house still remained in darkness. At last Obie turned to Uncle Oliver and me. "It's not the fuses," he announced. "It's the power. It must be off."

"Good heavens," said Uncle Oliver. "Are you sure, Obie?"

"I'm sure," Obie answered.

"We can't telephone for help," Uncle Oliver said, "so I suppose there's no way to get it fixed before tomorrow, at least."

"That's right," said Obie calmly.

Uncle Oliver made an effort and refrained from using language. "I don't know how I'm going to break the news to Mother, this time," he said.

We agreed that it was pretty bad.

Worse was to come.

10

FACES AT THE WINDOW

Obie was right. He usually is about things like that. The electricity in the entire house was off.

I thought that Aunt Claire took the news very well, considering everything.

All she said was "What are we going to do now?"

Obie replied very matter-of-factly, "We'll have to find candles and kerosene lamps."

"But where?"

He announced after a moment's thought, "I think I saw some old lamps down in the cellar."

Amanda and I went down after him. We rooted around, bumping against each other whenever the flashlight went out. Amanda let out a sudden shriek at one point, but it was only a cobweb.

Obie, of course, was right again. There were about half a dozen lamps sitting on a shelf. Luckily, they had good wicks and plenty of kerosene in them. When we brought them upstairs, Aunt Claire had lighted every candle she could find, and the rooms looked unfamiliar and wonderfully eerie. Everywhere you turned there were unexpected shadows filling the corners. There was a pleasant smell in the air, too.

"It's those bayberry candles I bought on Cape Cod last summer," Aunt Claire explained ruefully. "I was saving them for a special occasion."

"If this occasion isn't special I like to know what it is," Uncle Oliver told her.

Well, what with the candles and the lamps, the prospect, as well as the house, brightened considerably.

The next disaster area was the kitchen. The electric stove wouldn't work, of course, with the power off. Fortunately the refrigerator was gas.

"Oh dear," Aunt Claire said. "What will we do now, Mrs. MacMinnies?"

Mrs. MacMinnies, however, didn't seem one whit fazed.

"God's help is never farther than the door," she said. and she pointed toward the door of the shed. "I wouldn't go in there myself in the dark, not even if the Holy Father in Rome was to ask me, what with all the rats in there and all. But you, James, and you, Obie," she commanded, "you're to go in there please and bring out some kindling and some logs."

While we went after the logs and kindling she bustled about the big coal range. She was ready for us when we got back. Our arms ached with the loads we'd brought. "Just set them down," she ordered. In what seemed no time at all she had a real roarer going. We stood around and watched her admiringly. What's more, we were grateful for the heat. That stove really radiated.

"Don't just stand there like a living lump," Mrs.

MacMinnies said, handing me a brass hod. "I found this behind the stove. There ought to be some coal down in that cellar."

It wasn't any trouble finding the coal. When I lugged it upstairs, Mrs. MacMinnies stood beside the sink. Her face was longer than usual.

"I'm fashed this time," she announced. "There's no water coming out of the jig-ma-rig."

"Naturally," said Uncle Oliver. "The pump works by electricity too. I'm stumped. What do we do now?"

"And I did want a cup of tea," Mrs. MacMinnies said. "And the dear knows what I'll do for my hot-water bottle tonight. And how am I to get you all your suppers, please God!"

"And how will you children ever get your faces washed?" Aunt Claire exclaimed. "And your teeth brushed in the morning?" We were far from concerned, but Aunt Claire is very hygienic-minded.

Obie said with a snort, "That's easy enough."

We stared at him.

All he said then was "I'll want as many buckets and kettles as you can give me, Mrs. MacMinnies."

She looked at him as though he were demented, but she went and lined up a whole row of pails and deep pots and scrub buckets and such.

"That'll do for the time being," Obie said, nodding. He already had on his coat and galoshes, and he signaled me to do likewise. I did. Then he said, while I and everyone else stood mystified, "Take up your pail and follow me."

He grabbed the biggest bucket. I took another and followed him out to the porch, still wondering what he was up to.

Then I suddenly got the picture.

"Water water everywhere," Obie cried, waving his bucket at the tons of snow around us.

We filled all those buckets and things and set them on the stove.

"Well, I never," exclaimed Mrs. MacMinnies.

Amanda clapped her hands. "It's just like the Swiss Family Robinson," she cried.

Uncle Oliver regarded Obie proudly.

"Great minds," he said.

Obie said, "Really, Poppa, it was the most logical thing." Obie hates what he thinks of as unnecessary fussing.

"All the same," Uncle Oliver confessed sheepishly, "I would never have thought of that."

"Hal Sterling would have," Obie answered with a grin.

"Now, out of my kitchen the lot of you," Mrs. MacMinnies announced. "I'm going to make myself a cup of tea and then I have my work to do."

It wasn't until we went into the chilly living room that we realized the furnace was off too. So we built big fires in the fireplaces. Aunt Claire made us put on all the sweaters she could find, and extra socks.

Soon everything was surprisingly cheerful. Amanda was delighted. She said that it was just like olden times, and although Obie and I groaned because we felt she was about to wax poetic any minute, we secretly agreed with her. Uncle Oliver said he was exhausted from coping with everything and sank into his wing chair with a book. Aunt Claire went upstairs to worry about extra blankets, Mrs. MacMinnie creaked around in her steamy toasty kitchen, and Obie and I were fooling around with a kerosene lamp. We held sheets of paper over the glass chimney to see how close we could get them without singeing the paper.

After a while Sieglinde, grunting to herself, came pattering in to lie beside the fire. Then Maggie came inside too. I guess Mrs. MacMinnies had commanded her to come indoors. Out of the corner of my eye I could see her poke her long aristocratic nose hesitantly into the living room. After considering the matter for a time, she sniffed loudly and flumped down with a deep windy sigh beside the dachshund. I couldn't help thinking that she looked rather like a distinguished old lady in somebody's bedraggled old fur coat.

Soon Obie and I got bored with burning holes in Uncle Oliver's best manuscript paper. We drifted toward the window. Outside, our snowman stood like an ever-vigilant sentinel before the house. Around him the wind whistled, raising the snow from the ground and whipping it against the panes. We felt sort of sorry for poor old Abominable, being out in all that, but he didn't seem to mind. And he still had his hat on.

"Hey, Amanda," I called.

Obie threw her a disgusted glance.

"There's no sense trying to get her to do anything now," he muttered. "She's in the agonizing throes of poetic composition."

And so she was. She sat all scrunched up, paying no attention to anyone else. Now and again she licked her pencil and then stared up at the ceiling as though raking the heavens for inspiration. DeeDee was also being abnormally quiet, sprawled out in the middle of the rug, talking to herself in a private singsong.

Then Amanda stared about her in a startled kind of way and shook her head, so we knew that the creative fit was over.

Obie said, "Well?"

"Well what?" she answered warily.

"Well let's hear it. I know from the holy look on your mush that you've been composing an Ode to Springtime or a Meditation on a Dead Forget-me-not, or something like that."

Amanda tried to look offended, but we could see she was dying to read it to us.

She said slowly, "As a matter of fact, I was working on a poem about the Abominable Snowman."

Uncle Oliver shoved his book aside. "Let's hear it, Amanda," he said gently. I guess it must be some consolation to a writer to know that at least one of his children has inherited his literary talent, if in Amanda's case you can call it that.

"It's not anything, really," she said, suddenly turning shy. "It's very short."

"The shorter the better," Obie said.

Amanda didn't even bother to cast him a mean look. She put on a rapt expression and began:

> *"The Abominable Snowman*
> *Say some, does not exist.*
> *I know no man or woman*
> *Less likely to be missed."*

She paused.

"Is that all?" Obie asked, disappointed. Obie is hopeless about poetry. "Gunga Din" is just about his speed. But this time I could see his point. I mean, we both sort of felt left up in the air.

"I was going to add another bit about its living on the something something of faraway Tibet and no one's seen it yet," Amanda said defensively. "Of course it isn't polished."

Uncle Oliver stroked his chin.

"Let's have it again," he suggested.

We had it again.

"Hmm," Uncle Oliver murmured judicially, "very interesting. Very interesting indeed."

Just then there was a squeak from DeeDee.

"Poppa, I wrote a poem, too, and I want to recite it. Now."

"Wouldn't you prefer to wait until your mother and Mrs. MacMinnies come in, so that they too can be enchanted by it?"

"I'll tell it to them later." She stood up in the middle of the room. "'The Abdominable Snowman,'" she announced, "'by Diana Frederika Little.'" She stopped and looked around. "You're supposed to applaud now."

"When it's all over," Uncle Oliver told her, "we'll decide exactly how much acclamation your effort deserves."

DeeDee pursed her lips. "It's about the snowman we made outside," she resumed.

> *"Snowman, snowman, snowman,*
>   *I will call you Whitey.*
> *It makes me sad to see you stand*
>   *Outdoors in all that freezing cold without a nightie.*
>
> *Snowman, snowman, snowman,*
>   *Will you come and play?*
> *No, no, my pretty DeeDee. The sun is warm*
>   *And I'm afraid I will melt away."*

"Very nice," Uncle Oliver said.

Luckily, the rest of us were saved from having to make any comment by Aunt Claire's voice from the doorway.

"That was perfectly lovely, dear," she said. "And now supper's ready."

We had supper right there in the living room. Mrs. MacMinnies brought it in on trays and we ate by firelight and lamplight and candlelight. It was great, even though it was mostly leftovers from dinner, all except the lemon pie, because we'd finished the cake. And the pie went the way of the cake.

When we had washed the dishes with melted snow water, we sat around the fire again. No one was in a mood for ghost stories that night. I mean, what with the spooky lights and that wind shrieking outside, they would have seemed too real for comfort. As Uncle Oliver remarked, there is such a thing as having too much background atmosphere to a story. And because the power was off we couldn't turn on a radio to see what the weather was doing, and what had happened to the rest of the world outside Walkaway Hill.

So we just talked. It wasn't about anything in particular. And while Aunt Claire worried out loud about the telephone and the electricity and everybody's missing school the next day, I found myself wondering what the Old Man was doing all alone in the apartment, back in the city.

I guess fooling around in the snow must have made us tired, too, because before long we were yawning. Obie said, "Let's have a yawning contest," but we were too tired even for that. And yet we all felt a funny reluctance about going to bed. It wasn't just because of the cold rooms upstairs. It was as though we were waiting for something to happen, although we didn't know quite what.

Something did happen.

Amanda was beside the window, staring out at the snowman. I think she was trying to figure out an extra stanza for her poem. That was when she remarked to no one in particular, "It looks like a ghost, all alone out there."

"Whose ghost?" Obie sneered.

"It looks like the ghost of—of Mrs. Houghton!"

I glanced out over her shoulder.

I saw what Amanda meant. For a minute, in the clouded moonlight, in the middle of that endless stretch of white, with its mop wig and all, it did seem exactly as though it might be the specter of some eccentric old lady come back to haunt the house where she had lived all alone for so many years. But the snowman was all I saw. I smiled at the idea, thinking that if anyone were to think of such a thing, it would be Amanda, who loves to be dramatic. And yet the conviction suddenly seized me that something was out there: if not the ghost of Mrs. Houghton, then it was what I could only describe as a Presence.

Then Uncle Oliver said something—I forget what—and we moved away from the window.

We were on the point of putting out the lights and hiking up to those icy upstairs rooms when Maggie began to act up.

Her barking had been demented enough before, when she was outside, but I'd noticed that when she was in the house she always remained very quiet and, well, lady-like. Now, however, she dashed around the room, growling deep in her throat. Then she started to bark. I thought she had really gone out of her mind this time.

None of us knew quite what to make of it. After all, it can be pretty distracting when a great shaggy creature like Maggie behaves like something possessed, especially in a room where candles and firelight are flickering. It was creepy. I mean, it really was enough to set anyone's teeth on edge, let alone a bunch of people who had been through all the events of that weekend. So we just stood around uneasily, wishing we could figure out what was wrong this time, and trying to soothe her.

The more we tried to calm her down, the more excited she got.

"Och," said Mrs. MacMinnies, "it's probably the snapping of the log in the fire that's got her going now. Stop it at once, you mad creature!"

But it was obvious that there was more to it than that. Maggie was over at the windows by this time, barking her lungs out. Just to make things worse, Sieglinde took up the cry and yapped shrilly.

Uncle Oliver observed that it was quite a concert.

And then, suddenly, DeeDee let out a scream.

"What is it, darling?" Aunt Claire said.

"There's a face at the window!"

Aunt Claire shook her head. "Poor DeeDee," she said. "You're overtired."

"It's only the snowman, silly," Amanda told her.

"No it isn't!" DeeDee insisted. Her voice rose. "It's a face. I saw it."

"It can't be, you idiot," Obie said. "Nobody could get up here. We're snowbound."

DeeDee stared at him. Then her eyes traveled back to the window, reconsidering. They grew enormous. "There it is again. It is so somebody's face!"

Amanda ran to look. Then she gulped.

"Well?" Uncle Oliver said impatiently.

In an odd hushed voice Amanda said, "There was something there."

Obie said with a withering look, "It's probably the Abominable Snowman come all the way from the some-thing of Tibet, just to hear your poem about him." By now the dogs were frantic.

And then, simply to show Amanda and DeeDee how silly they were being, Obie went and peered out.

The next thing we knew, he had grabbed the flashlight and sprinted out to the front porch.

I was ready to scoot after him, but Aunt Claire called, "You stay right here, James," which took care of me.

We could see Obie's flashlight glimmering out in the snow, beaming all over the place. Aunt Claire marched briskly to the door. "Obie," she called in her no-nonsense voice, "I won't have you out there without a coat or anything. You're just begging for pneumonia." Then: "Get in here this instant."

Obie came in, reluctantly enough.

He had a queer glint in his eyes, I noticed, and he seemed odd and sort of pale. At the time, however, I figured it was just from coming in out of the cold and dark.

"Which was it," Uncle Oliver demanded with a wry smile, "the Abominable Snowman, or Mrs. Houghton's ghost?"

Obie said, "Neither."

He switched off the flashlight and tucked it under his arm. "It was nothing. Just those girls' imagination." But he didn't look at Amanda or DeeDee.

Aunt Claire declared that she didn't know what Obie thought he was doing. She said he ought to have known better, his chest being what it was.

Mrs. MacMinnies shook her head. "They've all gone stark out of their wits," she muttered. "It's moving to the country that's done it."

She got up, took a lamp, and went firmly out to the kitchen to fix her hot-water bottle. The rest of us fiddled around, blowing out candles and poking the fire to rest. The dogs finally calmed down, and Maggie settled uneasily on the WELCOME rug. She growled in her throat from time to time and kept her head alert, her ears pricked. Sieglinde, at her side, snored.

By the time we had trooped upstairs the house had turned noticeably colder. In the upper hall you could practically see your breath cloud up in front of your face.

Obie signaled to me when nobody was looking our way, so I waited for him by the bathroom door.

"All right," I whispered when he came up to me. "Spill it."

For a minute Obie didn't say anything. He just flicked the flashlight on and off. It gave me the creeps. Finally he said, "You know, there was somebody there."

I thought he was raving, or trying to see if he could scare me, and I told him so.

He shook his head solemnly.

"I swear I'm not fooling."

I was still dubious. And I still hoped that maybe Obie was just joking.

I said, "But you didn't actually *see* anyone, did you?"

He grabbed my sleeve. "That's the whole point, James. I did see somebody flapping around out there. DeeDee and Amanda were right. There was a face at the window."

"In all that snow, Obie? There couldn't have been anyone. You—you must have been seeing ghosts."

"Maybe so," he said shortly. He clutched my sleeve tighter. "But ghosts don't leave tracks, do they?"

"I—I'm not sure."

"Well, there were tracks in that snow, all right." I felt

my blood turn to ice. I somehow managed to stammer, "What—what kind of tracks?"

He frowned. "They were peculiar, not like a person's feet or boots or anything."

"Snowshoes? Skis?"

He shrugged. "I didn't have time to find out. Mamma was too worried about my sneezing or something. They could have been the Abominable Snowman's, for all I know. Anyway, we'll have to get up before everybody else and investigate."

"But—" I began. Then we looked at each other. I knew from the way he knitted his brows that Obie was really telling the truth.

11

TRACKS
IN THE SNOW

You can bet anything I didn't get much sleep that night.

After all, how could anyone have fallen asleep with everything so deathly quiet, with that terrible whiteness, brighter than moonlight, outside the window? Also, there was the paralyzing thought that someone or something was hanging around out there somewhere, leaving mysterious tracks like the Abominable Snowman's, tracks that weren't like anything human. I kept listening for I didn't know what, but I didn't hear a thing: only my own uneasy breathing.

I might add that it was no consolation at all to think that it was just like the things that happen in books. Frankly, I'd have preferred it to be a little less literary and a lot less scary. I found myself wishing that Obie were sleeping in the room with me. I even thought of getting up and stealing into his room, but I knew that if I did I'd never hear the end of it.

And so when Obie scrabbled lightly on my door I really felt relieved. I had never welcomed a morning so much in my life.

"What time is it?" I whispered.

"I'm not sure," he whispered back. "It's pretty early, though. The sun's already up, but it's still back of the hills."

Obie was already dressed. He waited, fidgeting, while I jumped into my clothes. My teeth chattered. We crept downstairs through the still house. Everyone else was still sleeping, even Mrs. MacMinnies.

Maggie got up and stretched when she saw us. She seemed glad to see us. She even wagged her tail in a tentative way.

It was warm in the kitchen where Mrs. MacMinnies had banked the fire in the big range. The rest of the house was grim. The chill was so thick, you could have scratched your initials into it. Obie and I didn't say a word to each other as we put on galoshes and sweaters and coats and mufflers.

Then we went out. The dogs went with us.

It was very quiet outside. The wind had died down at last and there was no stirring anywhere. It was like being behind a pane of thick glass, and the light had a strange color to it, sort of a dim purple. I sniffed the air. It had a fresh early smell that made my lungs hurt. Our snowman still stood there, the grin still visible where we had carved it on his face. The dogs disappeared, following some secret trail of their own. It was as though Obie and I were the only people awake in the whole world.

Suddenly, Obie touched my arm and pointed.

I looked.

Something dashed across the whiteness. At first I couldn't make out what it was. Then I saw that it was three deer: two big ones and a fawn. They flew past, bounding on those incredibly delicate legs of theirs, their velvety heads held high, their snowy scuts flashing. Then they were gone, as silently and as suddenly as they had appeared.

Obie, staring after them, whistled softly through his teeth. His eyes shone. But neither of us said a word. It was a wonderful thing to have seen, but there wasn't anything to say. It was just something to remember for always.

The stillness seemed to come alive after that. We noticed all sorts of things that hadn't been apparent before: chickadees calling in their shrill, insistent chirps, woodpeckers darting up the barks of the frosted trees, sparrows clouding the snow in forlorn groups. We saw at our feet the marks of their tiny feet, like hieroglyphics scrawled all over the snow's crust. We could see little trails where field mice or rabbits or some other small creatures had scurried, and the sharp slots the deer hoofs had left behind. I had never thought you could see so much in snow. It was like the fresh white page of a notebook.

Of the tracks Obie had seen the previous night, however, there was not a single sign.

"That's funny," he said, scratching his cheek.

"You must have imagined them, Obie," I told him.

He shook his head.

"I didn't imagine them, James," he said. "I tell you, I saw them, clear as anything."

"Well, there aren't any now."

He peered around in a dazed sort of way, trying to

figure out what had happened. Then he said, "I know. It's the wind."

"The wind?" I echoed, none too brightly.

He nodded.

"Sure," he said. "Look around you. The snow's drifted."

It was true. The blowing wind had changed everything overnight. High banks of snow now lay across parts of the tunnel we had dug, blocking it; and in places where we remembered that the snow had lain deep the day before, we could see that it now spread thinly over the ground, as though some enormous broom had swept it aside. Sections of the lane were almost bare, with the snow heaped mountainously high on the far side of it.

"Blast!" Obie said. "Wouldn't you just know it would happen? The clues are all gone. Wiped out."

It was pretty discouraging, but all the same we plunged out toward the lane to see if we could find anything.

There was nothing to be seen. The wind had been exasperatingly capricious. One minute we felt the hard earth practically under our feet. The next, we were flailing our way through a hip-high drift. The birds got noisier overhead. As the sun reached the crest of the hills, the snow's crust began to sparkle. But we weren't paying much attention to the morning anymore. We just plowed ahead, raking the powdery surface with our eyes and hoping to see those tracks—although we knew that it was about the most hopeless thing anyone could try to do.

We had worked our way about fifty yards down the lane when Obie abruptly halted. Then, with a shout of triumph, he waved me over to where he was bent nearly double over the windswept ground.

I punched a path through the drift that lay between us. "All right, Obie. What did you find?"

"Feast your old eyes on that, Dr. Watson" was all he said.

I dropped to my knees.

The snow there wasn't more than six inches or so in depth. It was a pocket that the wind had, somehow or other, failed to affect. And there were unmistakable tracks in it.

They were perfectly distinct. In fact, they were so clear and sharp, they might have been made that morning.

Only they weren't like any of the other tracks we'd seen.

They were nothing more than deep, perfectly straight dents in the snow. They went all the way down to the ground, so they must have been made by something with weight to it. Beyond that, they were absolutely baffling.

Obie was busy calculating.

"They're not more than about half a foot long," he muttered under his breath. "And they're very narrow. There's only one at a time. They're spaced about two or three feet apart. And from the look of them, there's no telling which way they're headed: if they're coming or going, that is."

"But Obie," I said, "what could have made them?"

"No animal, that's one sure thing. Can you figure how a human being could have made them, either?"

I said I was darned if I could.

"Inspect them carefully," he ordered. "It's not as though they were from skis or snowshoes or what have you, is it?"

I said, "Mmm," and tried to look intelligent.

"Come on, James," Obie said, excitement rising in his face. "Let's see how far they go."

Well, we followed those inexplicable tracks for about half a dozen yards. It was easy going and they were as plain to make out as you might wish. Then there just weren't any more. They ended as abruptly as they had begun. And that, I don't mind admitting, made me feel very nervous.

Obie wouldn't give up, so we floundered about in the area looking for more.

We didn't find any others, though. That was it.

"I think we've had it," Obie admitted at last.

At which point we noticed Mrs. MacMinnies flapping a dish towel at us from the kitchen window.

We started to backtrack. There was nothing else we could have done, unless we wanted to answer a lot of silly questions about what we had been looking for out there, et cetera, et cetera, which would have been fatal.

Anyway, Obie paused just before he reached the porch steps.

"What now?" I demanded, puffing.

He waited for me to catch up with him.

"Don't go saying anything to the others, James," he cautioned. "There isn't any sense getting them all worked up until we know more."

It sounded reasonable enough to me. In fact, it was exactly what I had been thinking. Amanda was excitable enough as it was, DeeDee was thoroughly unreliable, and there's never any knowing what grown-ups will do in the face of a crisis. "Right," I said.

Obie kicked stubbornly at a hardening drift. "All the same," he muttered, "I feel as though I ought to be able to make out what those tracks are." Obie hates to admit defeat.

I was about to make some lame answer when I saw him narrow his eyes.

"I'll figure it out yet," he said. "You wait and see."

I didn't bother to reply. I couldn't see how we were going to get around to solving that one all by ourselves.

Then we went inside.

12

WHITE MONDAY

As we'd expected, Mrs. MacMinnies was there in the kitchen shaking down the range. She was fully dressed. In fact, she was wearing enough sweaters to outfit a whole football eleven.

She stared sourly at us.

Now, Monday is generally supposed to be a blue day. "Blue Monday": that's what the Old Man and lots of other people are always saying. I suppose it's because the weekend is over and you have to go back to school.

This Monday at Walkaway Hill couldn't have been described as anything but stark white. And there was no question of anyone's having to go back to school. Even so, in the end it turned out to be a pretty blue day for all of us.

There's no need to depress you with the full details. For the record, however, it ought to be set down that it was Mrs. MacMinnies who started it off.

"Why anyone would bother to get up on a morning like this," she said, "is more than I can see." Then, "If I'm to get anyone's breakfast, I'll be needing more coal for the fire and more snow for water."

Obie and I went and got the coal and the snow.

When we brought it to her, she didn't even bother to thank us. She flung the coal into the stove. It hissed. Then she set the table for breakfast, rattling the dishes a good deal more than was necessary. Obie and I kept quiet. We'd learned long since that when Mrs. MacMinnies is enjoying one of her grumpy spells, the best thing is to let the hurricane ride its course.

But this time it was worse than any we'd witnessed before.

"If I ever get out of this place alive," she kept muttering to herself, "please God!" and more like that, always with a "please God!" at the end of it. When the table was set she directed a baleful finger toward the kitchen calendar.

"Who'd have believed it?" she said. "It's Saint Patrick's Day." She surveyed the forbidding landscape. "Look at that, now, will you? I ask you: Who's going to parade in the likes of that?"

Obie observed cheerfully, "Didn't your grandmother use to tell you 'If life hands you a lemon, make lemonade'?"

It was the wrong thing to say. Obie realized it the moment he uttered the words.

She turned on him in a rare fury.

"Things are bad enough around here without your being impertinent, Master Oliver B. Little, Junior," she snapped. "Lemon indeed!" She turned her face to the window again and shuddered. "It's more like a shroud."

We waited in grim silence for the others to come straggling downstairs.

Amanda was first.

She asked right off, "What were you two doing out there?"

I could have smacked her.

"Out where?" I asked uneasily.

Amanda assumed a stance of righteousness. "You know perfectly well where. I saw you through my window. You were acting awfully peculiar, as though you were looking for something."

Obie said, "As a matter of fact, we were."

"What?" Amanda demanded immediately, looking nauseatingly eager.

I signaled wildly to Obie behind Amanda's back, but he didn't even glance my way.

"If you must know," Obie told her loftily, "we were looking for inspiration. We're going into the poetry business!"

"I suppose," Amanda retorted spitefully, "that's why James is behaving like a windmill behind my back."

But that took care of Amanda—for a while, anyway.

Aunt Claire was the next one to come down. "The electricity isn't on down here by any chance?" she inquired. "Is it?"

Obie said of course it wasn't.

"That's what I was afraid of," she said. "It isn't on upstairs, either. And the telephone's still dead. Don't any of you dare to get sick!" She moved toward the window and regarded the thick whiteness with despair. Then, in a voice that startled me, it was such a sad, little girl's sort of voice, she said, "It doesn't look as though there'll ever be a garden out there, does it?"

I had to admit that it didn't.

Uncle Oliver loped in with DeeDee.

"Well, well!" he said in a hearty, pleased sort of way, rubbing his hands together cheerfully. "It's nice and warm in here!" Then he looked around at the lot of us.

"Hmm," he said. "My mistake."

Breakfast was more or less tense, with Mrs. MacMinnies slamming things down and saying, "Please God" through her teeth. Aunt Claire tried to help her, but that only made matters worse.

We scattered as soon as we decently could. Uncle Oliver put on an overcoat and wound a muffler around his neck and set off for his study to start a new chapter of *Hal Sterling*. Aunt Claire said she was going to lie down. DeeDee announced that she was going to make fancy dresses for Sieglinde and Maggie, and Mrs. MacMinnies wasted no time in whooshing Obie and Amanda and me right out of her kitchen.

"Go off and infest the rest of the house," she said.

So there we were.

Naturally, we had been beside ourselves with delight at the thought of having a free day from school without having to be sick or its being a holiday. But now that we had it, we didn't really know what to do with it. We should have been as merry as a pack of beagles, but we weren't. Don't ask me why. We didn't even feel like fooling around in the snow, although every one of us had had ideas about building forts and castles and whatnot, and having terrific snow battles. Finally, Amanda and I built a fire in the living room. Then we found books and settled down to read, huddled as close to the fireplace as we could get. Obie, however, was restless. I could tell because every time I glanced up from *Once Upon a Saturday*, I would catch him frowning through the windowpane at the place where we had seen those queer tracks.

The only ones who seemed to be enjoying the day to the full were the dogs. Unmindful of the dire fate that awaited them when DeeDee finished making those fancy clothes, Maggie and Sieglinde romped happily outside. Curiously enough, Maggie had left off barking. Once I looked out and saw her in the snow beside the porch. She glanced around to see if anyone was watching. Then she turned over on her back and wriggled around blissfully in the snow, her paws in the air. A moment later she had recovered herself and sat there as sedately as a dowager. The next time I looked out she was snoozing, with Sieglinde's sleek brown head resting on her flank. Just at that instant an icicle broke off the porch roof. It dropped straight down like a dagger, missing Maggie's side by an inch. All she did was to raise her head, look around her, growl faintly, and go back to sleep.

The morning dragged on its dreary length to lunch-time.

Mrs. MacMinnies had managed to scrape up a passable meal, considering the circumstances. We ate in the kitchen. It was pretty steamy there, but she still kept all her sweaters on.

Uncle Oliver descended looking out of sorts and scruffy.

"Did you get the new chapter off to a good start, dear?" Aunt Claire wanted to know.

"No," Uncle Oliver growled. "I did not."

"Oh, dear," Aunt Claire said. The rest of us looked down at our plates with sudden absorption, as though we'd never noticed their pattern before.

"I did not get a single line written," Uncle Oliver declared.

"What did you do, then, dear?"

He slapped the table, making all the glasses jump.

"This place is utterly distracting. It's worse than the city."

Mrs. MacMinnies stalked back to the stove with a look that spoke volumes.

"But what did you do, dear?" Aunt Claire insisted.

"If you must know," he burst out, "I spent all my time watching the birds fool around in the snow!"

We were all very much relieved when lunch was over.

Uncle Oliver stretched and sighed and said, "Well, try, try again," and departed for his study like Peary setting off for the North Pole. Aunt Claire said, "I suppose I ought to write some letters, but goodness knows when I'll ever get them down to the mailbox." Obie and Amanda and I had to go out and get more buckets of snow for Mrs. MacMinnies to melt down. DeeDee was all right: she had the dogs.

For Maggie and Sieglinde had come inside. Maggie even nuzzled DeeDee's hand. It was funny about Maggie: she was all fluffy and shiny now. The snow had done wonders to her coat. It was as though she'd had a complete dry-cleaning job. She practically looked like a different dog. And yet there was still something queer and nervous and reserved about her. She shied when any of us approached. But she followed DeeDee around like Mary's pet lamb, which made the rest of us furious. She even endured the ridiculous dressing-up that DeeDee submitted her to.

And so there we were again: Obie and Amanda and I, with nothing to do.

Boredom settled over us like the proverbial pall.

Suddenly Amanda jumped up. "I can't stand it any longer," she declared.

"Stand what?" Obie said, blinking.

Amanda made an impatient sweeping gesture, nearly knocking over one of Aunt Claire's favorite vases. "This!"

"Oh." And Obie went back to studying the sheet of notepaper on which he had made a diagram of the tracks.

"Could we do something, the three of us?" Amanda pleaded. "I mean, we have practically the whole house as our domain. We could organize a treasure hunt." Her eyes glittered. "Maybe we could find Mrs. Houghton's money!"

Obie nixed that suggestion with a glance of unutterable contempt.

"Or we could put on a play," Amanda suggested hopefully. Amanda always has been a great one for group efforts.

Obie shook his head.

"You'd be the director and the author and the star and everything. You always are when we do a play."

"Well, we ought to do *something*," Amanda maintained.

I was willing to go along, but Obie was still brooding over that diagram.

"You and James do something," he said. "Include me out."

Amanda's eyes narrowed with suspicion.

"Obie, you're up to something. I can feel it in my bones. You and James have a secret." Her voice turned coaxing. "Why don't you tell me what it is?"

To Obie's credit it ought to be said that he never lies. But when he's cornered he has a way of shoving the fatal question to one side, so that he doesn't have to tell the truth, exactly, either.

He answered cautiously, "What could we possibly be up to?"

"That's the trouble," Amanda replied. "I don't know."

"What you don't know won't hurt you."

"I detest, hate and despise secrets!"

"Only when you're not in on them," Obie sneered.

Well, one word led to another. And that's how the fight began.

Mrs. MacMinnies marched in from the kitchen, grim-faced, and broke it up.

"Well?" she demanded, her hands spread on her hips and one shoe tapping the floor.

"Obie called me a creep and an ugly mutt," Amanda declared with passion. "And I wouldn't dream of repeating the rest of it."

"She called me a pig," Obie retorted sullenly. "And that wasn't all she called me, not by a long shot."

"Compliments pass when the quality meet," Mrs. MacMinnies observed. And she set us to fetching more wood for the fireplace, and coal for the stove, so at least we were united again, against her.

Not long after that Uncle Oliver returned from the North Pole, with Aunt Claire in his wake,

"I can't work up there," he complained. "It's too lonely."

Aunt Claire said, "You ought to know by now that being a writer is a lonely job."

"I do. And I wish I were a headwaiter or a bus driver or a dogcatcher, or something less bleak," he declared. "Furthermore, it's very distracting not knowing what's going on in the world. What do you expect me to do with no newspapers, no mail, no radio, no telephone, and no way to get out?"

"Oliver, really. That's why you wanted to move to the country: to avoid all that. I wish you wouldn't be so inconsistent."

"At least," he said, in his most ironic voice, "allow me to be inconsistent in my own home."

Aunt Claire cast her eyes to the ceiling.

Uncle Oliver considered.

"I'm getting stir-crazy, that's what," he declared. He surveyed us. "What are you all up to?"

"Nothing much," Obie said.

"Then you could at least keep the fire going," he grumbled. "It's practically out."

"We were trying to save the logs for tonight," I explained. "The woodpile is getting low."

"Oh," Uncle Oliver said. Then he brightened. "We'll have to make Nova Scotia knots."

We all, including Aunt Claire, looked perfectly blank.

"I learned how to make them when I was doing research for *Hal Sterling: Boy Mountie*," he said. "Get me some old newspapers."

We scurried and got them.

"This is how you do it." He took one section, divided it into smaller sections of three or four sheets each. Then he folded them the long way several times, until each section was a thin belt. "Now you simply make a knot," he explained, doing so. "It burns like billy-o. And it lasts."

We watched the knots take fire. He was right. They burned evenly and gave out a lot of heat, just like wood.

The Nova Scotia knots provided some distraction. We were all too busy making them to notice how unusually quiet everything was. There was no wind anymore. Maggie was calm for a change, and a thick peace hung over the house and over Walkaway Hill.

Which is why what happened after that seemed so especially peculiar.

It had grown dark sooner than you would have

expected. Or maybe it was that being in the country you just noticed the darkness right away. It wasn't like summer, when there's a long dusk. One minute it was late afternoon, with the sun like a dying fire between the skeleton trees. And the next thing you knew, the windows were already black squares and the house itself was suddenly turned into a robber's cave of darkness. We were busy getting the candles and the kerosene lamps ready for another evening of no electricity when, before we knew what had taken place, the whole house blazed startlingly into light.

It was just like a tremendous birthday cake.

And then the faucets all gushed water, and Mrs. MacMinnies's radio blared in the kitchen, and, with a low roar, the furnace went on.

After the first shock of astonishment we all started to laugh. It was as though all our gloom and ill temper and boredom and everything were dispelled with the coming back of the electric power. The house had come alive again. So had we. We laughed as we sprinted to turn off the faucets and switch off the lights we didn't need. And we were still laughing, our hearts miraculously and suddenly light, as we started to put away the candles and the lamps.

Aunt Claire ran to try the telephone. It was still dead, but it didn't seem to matter quite so much anymore.

And then, just like a giant's birthday cake, all the lights went out again in one breath. And the radio and the furnace stopped the same instant.

Obie happened to be standing beside me then. Through the returned darkness I could make out his face. It was white and perplexed.

"That's very funny," he said. But his voice was grim.

DeeDee started to wail, naturally.

Uncle Oliver used language, and the rest of us held our breath, wondering if the lights would come on again.

They did, almost immediately.

We stood there blinking dazedly at each other.

Then they went off a second time.

I had a funny feeling, right down the length of my spine, that somebody else, a stranger, was in the house. I couldn't explain to myself why I thought so, but I was so convinced of that uninvited extra presence that I didn't dare to turn around and look.

I counted to ten.

Then I counted to twenty.

But this time the lights stayed off.

We were plunged back into gloom as well as darkness. It was as though we were too paralyzed even to get the candles and the lamps again. But we did.

All during the meal that followed, Obie was strangely silent. We chattered away, speculating on what had caused the current to behave in such an odd fashion, but Obie didn't join in. When I tried to catch his eye, he avoided mine. And his frown had deepened into a scowl.

We didn't do much that night. After the dishes were done, we just sat and wondered what was going on in the world outside. And we all went up to bed early. Mrs. MacMinnies said, mostly to herself but loudly enough for the rest of us to hear, "No wonder that the poor soul who lived here died. It's enough to kill a saint!" She went to her room clutching her hot-water bottle, and her door slammed behind her with terrible finality.

I was in bed, huddled under the blankets and thinking about those tracks and the strange way the lights had acted, and all the odd events that had occurred so far at Walkaway Hill, when I heard, low and tentative, the creaking of hinges.

I was too terrified even to yell.

The door opened slowly. I just lay there, staring at the widening gap, my teeth rattling in my face.

Someone was in the room now, coming toward my bed.

I cowered. My blood turned to ice water.

Then I saw that it was Obie.

"I didn't mean to scare you, James," he said.

"You—you didn't scare me," I lied.

"I didn't want Amanda to hear me," he explained. "She's still awake, reading, in her room."

"Well?" I said.

"It's about those lights."

"What about the lights?"

"I've been thinking," Obie said. "And I'm sure now that they had something to do with those tracks."

"How do you figure that one out?" I asked.

He shrugged.

"I can't figure it out," he said earnestly, "but I just know that it's so. I'll know for sure in the morning."

"How?"

He looked mysterious. "I'm going to carry on a little independent investigation. Will you help, James?"

"Of course I'll help," I said. "But what are you going to do?"

"You'll see tomorrow," he said. And before I could ask any more questions, the door creaked shut. He was gone, leaving me there alone in the ominous darkness with my thoughts.

13

THREE THIRDS OF A GHOST

It wasn't exactly easy, the next morning, sneaking off for Obie's private investigation. Reconnoitering, he called it. It was well after breakfast before we finally managed to elude Amanda's watchful eye and the unwanted notice of everyone else. Even so, it was a wonder we did it at all.

We couldn't get past the dogs, though.

Maggie, for some reason, wanted to go with us. And since wherever Maggie went, Sieglinde stuck to her like a tick, we had to let her come along as well.

Obie said it was better that way. If anyone were to catch a glimpse of us through a window, it would look as though we were off for a perfectly innocent trudge through the snow.

It was a clear day. The sun was out, sparkling all over everything. The Abominable Snowman grinned stoically as we passed him. The whiteness was fairly blinding, but after a little while we got used to it. And though the wind hadn't entirely died down, it was a lot less insistent than it had been. For one thing, the snow devils had stopped whirling.

It shook me to find that yesterday's tracks were gone, erased by the wind. Obie didn't seem surprised. He merely grunted at the faintly dented place in the snow's surface that indicated where they had been.

Altogether, Obie didn't say much, which was rather disconcerting. After all, I couldn't help thinking that, since he'd asked me to come along, he might explain what he was up to. But he only kept glancing overhead, muttering to himself under his breath and kicking his way through the heavy drifts.

I floundered after him.

Finally, I couldn't stand it a second longer.

"Where are we going, Obie?" I demanded.

He said through his teeth, "You'll see soon enough."

"I don't get it," I said. "We seem to be heading down the lane."

"Are we?" was all he said.

So I gave up and just followed along silently, wishing he were a bit less taciturn. Everything was so very still, though, that I couldn't help feeling a little apprehensive. Even our galoshes treading in the snow seemed terribly loud in all the quietness that surrounded us like a glass globe.

Suddenly, Obie said, more to himself than anything, "There. I thought so."

He stood still and pointed to the electric wires strung far over our heads. They stretched in stark black lines from one pole to the next, like long pencil-marks drawn across the clear sky.

"Do you see that, James?"

I nodded, wondering what was so special about it.

"There doesn't seem to be any break in them along here, does there?"

I admitted, after a moment's squinting, that there didn't.

"There's no ice on them so far as you can see, is there?"

"No," I said.

"All right. Now just tell me where the lines lead to."

I followed them with my eyes.

"That's easy," I replied. "They seem to lead straight down to the barn."

"Right," he said. "And that's where we're going now."

I supposed Obie must have noticed my hesitation because he said with a wry smile, "You're not worried about the deep snow, are you, James?"

"Of course not," I answered. "I don't mind the snow at all."

His eyes narrowed under the peak of his cap.

"Then what's making you so nervous? It isn't the barn, is it?"

"Well," I said, gulping, "not exactly."

Obie groaned. "You're just like Amanda. You probably expect to see skeleton claws all dripping with blood, and sheeted ghosts and I don't know what all. Don't you?"

I didn't answer that one. It was a little too close to the truth. After our first experience with the barn, and all the other things that had happened since, I couldn't help being a bit jittery. I wasn't exactly sure why, but I was.

Obie made an impatient gesture. "The trouble with you and Amanda," he declared, "is that you're both too literary. You've read too many books."

"It's not that," I began. "It's only—"

"Only what?" he scoffed. "Don't tell me now that you really believe in ghosts!"

"Well," I said slowly, "you never can tell about things like that."

He groaned again.

I disregarded it.

"Anyway," he said, "we're going into that barn, because it's where the power lines lead to. If you're afraid to come with me, you can turn back now. I can go by myself."

I pressed my lips together firmly. "I'm going with you, Obie."

He grinned. I grinned back at him. And then we forged ahead.

It wasn't the easiest thing in the world plunging through those high drifts. Several times we tumbled and went flying tail over breakfast time. The dogs charged along beside us, their noses and eyebrows all white from sniffing after rabbits. They seemed to be enjoying the expedition. Once, when we fell, Maggie even came and stood over us, licking our faces. Eventually we made it. We were right within a few yards of the barn's huge red door.

All the time Obie had been looking up to the electric wires. There wasn't a single break in them, up to the point where they entered the barn.

Obie surveyed the snow that had blown against the door.

"What are you looking for now?" I demanded.

"I wondered if there might be any tracks around here," he answered thoughtfully. "I don't see any, though. The wind's been blowing so, that even if there were tracks they'd be covered up by now."

He kept looking anyway. And suddenly he let out a muffled yell.

I looked up.

Obie was holding something in his hand.

"What did you find?" I asked, running up to him.

"These," he said, and he showed me what looked like a pair of oddly contrived sticks. There were bits of cord dangling from them. He turned them over. "Queer," he said to himself. "I wish I knew what they are."

"They're only pieces of wood," I said. "They're not anything."

He shook his head. "They're more than that," he said solemnly. He examined them once more before he stuffed them inside his jacket. "I'll figure that one out later," he said. "We're going inside the barn now."

As we turned to the barn door, Maggie drew back and snarled. She looked positively savage, but we were much too interested in what we were doing to pay any heed to her, even when she started to bark. Sieglinde began yapping hysterically, but we figured that it was just to keep Maggie company.

We saw then that the barn had two doors. There was the great big one that we had used the other time, and near it, swinging idly back and forth on its hinges, was a much smaller door, just large enough for a man to pass through.

"I didn't spot that one before," Obie said.

"Neither did I. It must have been there, though."

As we stared at it, the wind swept it wildly open and banged it against the side of the barn.

We peered across the sill. Powdery snow had drifted onto the floorboards.

Obie's brow furrowed. "At any rate, it wasn't open the last time."

"Maybe the wind did it during the storm," I suggested hopefully.

"Maybe," he said. "And maybe not."

The barn's interior loomed before us, dark and shadowy even in that bright daylight. The emptiness was enormous.

"Come on," Obie said.

Maggie's barking was even louder and more desperate than before. I stood hesitating for just a moment. Obie looked over his shoulder at me in an odd way.

Then I followed him inside.

He was already circling the vast room, surveying the bare inside walls in a businesslike manner.

"What are you searching for now, Obie?" I asked.

"A switch, naturally," he replied. "I looked all over the house for the main power switch. There wasn't one. So I figure it ought to be down here."

I was still puzzled.

"What difference would that make, since the storm knocked the power out?"

Obie gave me a pitying look.

"Because," he said, "I suspect that the current didn't go off because of the storm."

I must still have looked pretty blank.

"And," he added, "it didn't go off by itself."

"Then how—?"

Obie's eyes stopped raking the walls and turned full on me.

"I think someone must have turned it off deliberately," he said.

It was getting to be too much for me. "But why?" I insisted.

"That's for us to find out," he said.

I was getting queasier by the minute. The boards of

the floor creaked under our feet. The barn smelled strange and musty, the door kept banging against the side, and my feet were cold. Furthermore, Maggie was acting up very oddly. She was barking as wildly now as she had the first day I came to Walkaway Hill. Her hackles stood up. She wouldn't come within yards of the threshold. In fact, she was racing back and forth in a half circle around the door as though to warn us away.

Obie suddenly said, "I thought so!"

"What have you found now?" I did my best to keep the words from sounding shaky.

"The switch, stupid." Obie said in a low triumphant voice. He dragged an old crate over to the wall, jumped on it, and stood facing a black metal box which I would certainly never have noticed. It was placed high up against a beam. "Watch this," Obie said as he yanked a lever.

A light went on, near the ceiling.

He was about to jump down when I called, "Look out, Obie!"

It was a good thing I had seen it in time. Another second and Obie would have had it, for right beside the spot where the crate now stood, something yawned. I could spot it then because a light glimmered faintly from somewhere in the depths.

Obie came down on the safe side and together we advanced to investigate.

It was an open trapdoor. Near it, a bare bulb swung, illuminating a fixed ladder and not much else.

We stared at the opening. There was nothing to be seen so we lay on the floor and peered down. The bulb was so weak that we could make out hardly anything.

"Well?" said Obie. "What are we waiting for?"

"Where are you going?" I whispered.

"Down those rungs," he whispered back. "I want to see what's at the bottom."

I'm not exactly a coward, but I think there are times when one ought to be cautious. I knew this was one of them.

I got to my feet very slowly.

"Are you coming, James?"

"Yes," I said at last. "But you go first."

Obie made his way down the ladder and I went after him.

We found ourselves in a long, low room. The concrete floor was hard and cold. We stood side by side squinting into the gloom. The naked bulb circled at the end of its cord. It was a minute or so before we could take in anything of what lay around us.

The place was a mess. There were empty cans heaped at our feet and an indescribably unhealthy smell hung over everything. It reminded me of something, but at the moment I was so jumpy that I couldn't remember what.

"Somebody's been here," Obie whispered. "Recently."

"Somebody's still here," I whispered back. The hair along the back of my neck was standing up. "I can feel it, Obie."

"Nuts," Obie said firmly, and strode forward.

The light bulb swung in a wild and lurid curve, flickering.

In a harsh whisper Obie said, "Who's there?"

I just stood and shivered in my galoshes. I couldn't help it.

There was no answer.

The silence must have given Obie courage. He raised his voice. "Who's down here? Come forth and show yourself, whoever you are!"

There was no reply this time either.

All of a sudden Obie jumped backward. He grabbed at my sleeve. His face was pale.

"James," he breathed in my ear, "look!"

I managed to stammer out the single word: "Where?"

"Right there, near your foot."

I didn't want to look, but I had to.

There, on some bales of dirty hay, lay a figure. It looked like a man's body and it was spread out over those bales like a Saint Andrew's cross.

In a voice that went through me like the chill of death, Obie said, "There's your ghost, all three thirds of him."

We stood there holding on to each other. Neither of us could move. Our feet seemed to have frozen fast to the cement of that icy floor.

The ghost raised its head and groaned.

That was all we needed. Obie and I went up that ladder in record time. I don't remember now which one of us scaled it first. We tore out of that barn as though a legion of clawlike hands, all dripping with blood, were clutching at us.

We hurled ourselves blindly out into the snow. The door waved back and forth, making an eerie creaking sound behind us, but we didn't stop to put down the latch.

Maggie growled as she ran alongside me, and Sieglinde yipped frantically. It was as if they knew what we had encountered down there.

I stumbled and fell, pulling Obie down with me. We picked ourselves out of the drift, blew the cold snow out of our faces, and pelted up the lane in panic.

We didn't stop then until we were halfway to the house. We had to halt at last because neither of us had a gulp of breath left. I felt as though someone had stuck a dagger into my side.

We flopped, gasping, onto a snowbank.

We lay there and looked at each other.

I was the first to speak.

"Well, Obie, what are we going to do now?"

"I don't know," he confessed.

"I think we ought to go to Uncle Oliver and tell him," I said.

"Not on your life. We're going to handle this one ourselves."

"But how?"

Obie was thoughtful.

"Now that we've discovered the ghost," he said finally, "we'll have to figure out some way to find out who he is and what he's doing here."

I felt dubious, and I know I must have shown it.

But by this time Obie had caught his second wind.

"Listen, James," he said urgently. "Did you notice if he had any weapons?"

"Weapons?" I repeated in a strangled voice.

"Knives, guns, anything like that," Obie said impatiently.

"No."

"No weapons? Or no, you didn't see?"

"I didn't see."

"What did you see?"

I told the truth. "Not much," I said.

Obie's tone turned cross. "Why didn't you look while you were there?"

"Why didn't you? You were closer."

He frowned. "I did see something," he said slowly. "Let me think. I remember that it looked like a grown man, and his face was dark and scruffy, as though he hadn't shaved in weeks, and his hair was all matted and tousled. And there was something else."

"Blood?" I ventured, swallowing hard.

"I don't think so. No. There was something lying beside him." He closed his eyes for a moment, recollecting. "I know: it was an old potato sack. Only it had holes cut out of it, like a mask."

"What?"

"You heard me."

"Then Amanda was right, after all."

Obie looked as though he'd been hit by lightning.

"Of course she was! That's what she saw before you came, only I convinced her she was imagining things. And it must have been his footsteps, too, that she heard. Something ominous was really going on all the time."

"Well, you owe Amanda an apology."

"I guess I do."

"Obie."

"Yes?"

"Do you think he was—dead?"

"No," Obie said. "Definitely not. He couldn't have been. He groaned, didn't he?"

"That's true," I said. "Maybe he was sick and needed help."

"Hmm," Obie said. He packed a snowball and sent it flying toward Maggie. "Oh, be quiet, Maggie," he snapped. "I'm trying to think, and I can't, not while you're barking all the time."

Maggie edged away, Sieglinde after her, but she was still howling in a way that would have given goose pimples to a corpse. I listened, getting edgier by the minute.

"Then there were these," Obie said, pulling those queer wooden objects out of his jacket.

"What do you think they can be?"

"Darned if I know." He rubbed his cheek as he turned

the bits of wood over and over. "I wish I could make them out. I'm sure they have something important to do with the case." He flicked them this way and that, concentrating all the while. I looked on helplessly.

Suddenly Obie said, "Look at this!" and stuck one of them in the snow's crust.

It made exactly the same indentation as the ones we had tracked the day before.

"Stilts!" Obie exclaimed. "I should have thought of that. They're a kind of homemade stilts!"

My jaw dropped.

"But why were they lying outside the barn?" Then I saw light. "He must have been using them so that no one could follow his footprints."

"Right," Obie said. "He must have been trying to get into the house. No, wait a minute. I think he just wanted to scare us. That must be what his game was."

"But why would anyone want to do that, Obie?"

"That," he said, "is what we'll have to find out before we can go any further." He shoved the crude stilts back inside his jacket. "I'm going to have to do a lot of figuring in the next hour or two," he said significantly.

We hauled ourselves out of that bank and stole back toward the house.

Maggie was still nervous and twitchy. Although we called her, time and again, she was too leery to venture near either of us.

"Let her be, Obie," I said. "I have a hunch that she won't calm down until that ghost in the barn is laid. I think that's probably what was bothering her all along."

Obie nodded.

"Maybe," I suggested cautiously, "we ought to tell Amanda about it."

Obie said, "Don't be ridiculous, James."

"We can't capture a ghost all by ourselves," I told him.

"Why not? Anyway, Amanda's a girl."

"But Obie, after all—"

I found myself standing there all alone. Obie had abruptly left me and was scrutinizing the side of the house, over by the far kitchen window. I couldn't help smiling to myself. He looked exactly like Sherlock Holmes, only without the magnifying glass and the deerstalker hat.

I raced over to him.

"What now?" I demanded.

He regarded me grimly.

"The telephone, James," he said. "Look at this: the wires have been cut, right here. I should have thought of it before."

"I think we really ought to tell Uncle Oliver now," I said.

"Oh, shut up for a minute, will you?" Obie said brusquely. "This is serious business. I'm thinking."

"Genius at work," I muttered in my most sarcastic voice.

Obie's look was withering.

I shut up.

14

A VISITOR FROM OUTER SPACE

Obie and I did our best to walk into the house as though nothing out of the ordinary had happened to us.

We needn't have bothered.

Nobody noticed us. Simply because the electricity was working again, everyone was too excited to pay the least attention to our return.

They were all in the kitchen.

I don't think they had even realized we had gone out, except for Amanda, who looked up slyly from her notebook and darted a suspicious glance in our direction. Then she tossed her mane and went back to committing a deathless lyric to paper.

We could hear the comfortable low roar of the furnace, as though a genial lion were down there in the cellar and had just awakened, purring. The house had already begun to thaw out. At least, the edge of the long chill had gone.

Uncle Oliver sat on the edge of a chair, his ear to the radio, catching up on the news. Aunt Claire was jiggling the telephone.

"It still doesn't work," she announced, looking concerned.

Obie jabbed me in the side to keep me from blurting out anything about the wires having been cut—as though I didn't have sense enough to keep my jaws clamped right then.

Aunt Claire set down the receiver. She said, "I hope at least that the electricity is going to stay with us for good, this time."

"I think it will, now," said Obie calmly.

Aunt Claire regarded him a little oddly. She was about to say something, but just at that moment she remembered about the hot water and ran to try the tap.

Uncle Oliver snapped off the radio. "You'll have enough hot water for several baths. Just be patient and give the heater a modicum of time."

"Oh," she said. Then: "Was there any news, dear?"

"Nothing special, except that the snow was a lot worse upstate. They're still burrowing their way out from under I don't know how many inches of it. Otherwise, the world seems to have gotten along pretty well without us." He seemed somewhat disappointed.

"The world may have gotten along nicely enough without me," Mrs. MacMinnies cut in, "but I'm not going to get along without the world from now on, please God. If you asked me," she added, underlining her comment with a sniff, "there's more than one way to be buried alive."

"Never mind, Mrs. MacMinnies," Uncle Oliver said jovially. "The Marines'll be along any day now to shovel us out."

"Marines or no Marines," she retorted, "we're running low on supplies. There'll be no milk left by suppertime. So much for your gracious country living."

As for DeeDee, it was as plain to see as the snow all around us that she had been wild with boredom all morning, and was still at loose ends. I recognized the look in her eye. She was longing for some attention, animal or human.

Just then she caught a glimpse of Sieglinde's tail, waving out of a snowbank.

She rushed to the porch door. "There you are now," she called. "Sieglinde, you come right in here!"

Sieglinde refused to budge without Maggie, and Maggie did not seem at all interested in coming indoors. The dachshund emerged from the snowbank, frosted up to her eyebrows, blinked at DeeDee, and then dashed into another snowbank.

DeeDee stamped her foot.

"She's always with that Maggie," she complained. "Doesn't she know that she's mine? I want her to come in and play with me."

"Och," Mrs. MacMinnies said contemptuously, "that dog'd be the slave of anyone who'd bother to feed her all day long."

DeeDee pouted, but Sieglinde remained outside, snuffling through the snow with Maggie.

"And now out of here, the lot of you," Mrs. MacMinnies said. "I'll use my lungs when the meal is ready."

Lunch, for a change, was a pretty lively affair. Uncle Oliver cracked a lot of jokes, mostly so bad that we couldn't help laughing at them. No one except me noticed the cloud on Obie's face, and of course I didn't count. I knew that he was busy thinking, and I was anxious to know if he had arrived at any conclusions or decisions. But the one time I looked his way and caught his eye, he shook his head.

I felt understandably nervous. I knew we didn't have too much time. There was no guessing what our ghost would do next.

Well, lunch was over, finally. Uncle Oliver retired to wangle Hal Sterling out of his current dire predicament. He appeared very cheerful about it, which was a relief to us all. It's no fun, I can tell you, having a brooding, glowering author wandering around the house. Aunt Claire went up to enjoy a bath. "I hope nothing happens now," she said. "I'm going to soak in that lovely hot water for hours." The younger generation had to stay around and help Mrs. MacMinnies with the dishes.

Mrs. MacMinnies swished a mountain of soapsuds in the sink. "When all this is over," she said, "I'm going back to living like folks, please God."

Amanda set down the platter she'd been wiping and looked solemnly at her. "Mrs. MacMinnies," Amanda said.

"What is it now?"

"Why do you always say 'please God'?"

Mrs. MacMinnies deliberately dried her hands on her apron. Then she folded her arms. We were all watching her and waiting to hear what she would say.

"I always say 'please God' when it's anything to do with the future," she answered quietly. "After all, everything is in His hands, and whatever happens, it's God's will. So what else could you say but 'please God'? There now. I hope that answers your question."

Amanda nodded gravely. "I think it's a perfectly lovely thing to say," she replied.

"I'm glad you approve," Mrs. MacMinnies remarked with a twitch of her steely lips. "And now get on with your drying. I want to have some time to myself today, please God."

We had just about finished stashing the dishes away, and I was on the point of cornering Obie in the pantry to ask him what we were going to do now about that ghost in the barn, when Mrs. MacMinnies suddenly let out a piercing shriek.

That sound was, to say the least, one of the most bloodcurdling I had ever heard in my whole life.

Then I realized that for some time the dogs had been barking dementedly outside.

Obie and I sprinted back to the kitchen.

Mrs. MacMinnies stood like a marble statue beside the sink. Amanda and DeeDee clung to her. All three of them were ashen-faced, staring at the porch door as though they'd beheld a specter.

Obie and I turned our heads toward the door. My legs suddenly felt like boiled spaghetti.

There was a dark shadow, motionless against the glass section of that door.

The shadow formed the outlines of a man's head and shoulders.

Obie and I were too stiff with alarm to do anything but stand there like a couple of dummies from the waxworks.

The door slowly began to open.

Mrs. MacMinnies shrieked again.

A foot with a heavy rubber boot on it appeared in the opening. A moment afterward a gloved hand waggled its way groping into the room.

Not one of us dared to budge.

Then, in what seemed to me to be the tones of one lately risen from the sepulcher, a voice on the other side of that door cried, "Help me, someone, for heaven's sake!"

It was a dreadful moment.

Obie was the only one in the room with sense enough to do anything.

He seized a knife from the table. While the rest of us watched in horror, he strode forward. Amanda cried out, "Obie, don't!" But it was too late. He gave the knob a sudden jerk and yanked the door open all the way.

I gasped.

It was as though we were confronted by a visitor from Outer Space, a traveler from some other planet.

Obie stepped back.

The figure that filled the frame of the doorway was tall and terribly thin. He wore high boots and a checked lumber jacket. A bright red hunter's cap was pulled down over his eyes. His face was almost entirely covered with a scarf. And in his arms he bore an enormous bulging brown paper sack.

Obie's jaw dropped.

"It's Charlie Murofino!" he cried.

As so it was. For a couple of seconds we were all too tense to do anything. Then Obie began to laugh, and the rest of us joined in, laughing wildly, hysterically, frantically, so that our sides hurt with the effort. Mrs. MacMinnies stood by the sink fanning her face with her apron. "God's help is never farther than the door," she declared between gasps.

Charlie gawped at us in bewilderment.

"What in—" he began. Then, "Here," he commanded. "Somebody take this load of stuff. My arms are stiff."

I took the paper bag and set it on the table.

He blinked at us, obviously thinking we were as crazy as a pack of hyenas.

"Where's your father?" he asked Amanda.

"Upstairs, working on his book," she managed to

reply. "Tappity-tap-tap. We're not allowed to disturb him." Her gasps subsided to an inane giggle.

"Oh. Where's your mother then?"

"She's taking a bath," DeeDee announced. "I'll go and get her right now."

"That won't be necessary," Charlie assured her hastily. He indicated the bag. "I thought you'd need some stuff, so I brought up a lot of eggs and milk and bread and things like that. And the newspapers."

Mrs. MacMinnies had recovered her composure.

"You go right out again and wipe your wet boots off on the mat," she ordered. "I won't have anyone tracking up my clean kitchen with all that filthy snow."

"Yes, ma'am," Charlie said meekly, and went outside. While he stamped off the snow, Mrs. MacMinnies poured him a mugful of hot coffee, cut a thick wedge out of a pie we hadn't seen before, and set it out on the table.

Charlie came back into the house grinning.

"You women are all alike," he said.

Mrs. MacMinnies merely pulled out a chair and said, "Sit down now and drink your coffee and eat that pie."

"Yes, ma'am," he replied, and we watched while he gulped his coffee and engulfed the pie.

Mrs. MacMinnies stood by the table surveying him in wonder.

"The blessed man!" she exclaimed. "And the dear knows how he got here."

"Walked," Charlie said.

Mrs. MacMinnies crossed herself.

"Walked? In all that?"

"'Twasn't too hard," he said. "I left the truck down on the road. The road's clear, at least. Then I walked my way up your lane. It's drifted pretty bad, but you can do anything, providing you have the right equipment."

Obie and I eyed those high rubber boots with open envy.

Charlie pushed away his empty plate. Without a word Mrs. MacMinnies loaded it with another generous slab of pie.

"Thank you, ma'am," he said with an even wider grin than before. "Best pie I've eaten since I don't know when." It disappeared in two forkfuls, and I will say that none of us begrudged it to him.

He let out a loud sigh and leaned back in his chair.

"Well," he demanded, "how was it?"

Then we all started talking at once. Everything poured out in a flood of babble—everything, that is, except for the most important things. Obie and I didn't dare mention them in front of the others. Charlie listened until it was all said, and we stood looking at him and feeling queerly empty now that we'd told him.

Mrs. MacMinnies said, "Och, you don't know how good it is, after so long, to see another human soul from the world outside."

I nodded. She was dead right. I hadn't realized myself how good it would be, actually, to see Charlie Murofino again.

Charlie said, "Anyway, you seem to have managed all right, like a real bunch of old-timers. It's been rough on everybody, this fall of snow, coming so late and all. To tell the truth, I was worried about all of you, being newcomers, and stuck this way on the hill. Fact is, I tried to get you on the phone about twenty times. All I ever got was a busy signal. You must have been talking on that thing day and night."

"No, we weren't," Amanda said. "The thing's on the blink. It hasn't been working at all since the storm."

"Oh," he said mildly. "That's funny."

"But the electricity's back on again. It went on this morning."

He knitted his thick eyebrows. "That's very funny."

"Why?" Amanda wanted to know.

"Like I said, it was a pretty heavy snowfall. But nobody else's power lines broke, so far's I know. And nobody else's phone went out. Not that I heard of, anyhow."

"Well, ours did," Amanda said, as though it were something to be proud of.

Obie's eyes shifted uneasily toward me. I shrugged.

Charlie stretched. He pulled on his gloves. "I got to be going," he said. "I just wanted to run up here and see if you were all right. Soon's I reach home I'll get on to the phone company and tell them your line's out of order. And tell Mrs. Little she can pay me back for those groceries and things some other time."

"What I want to know," said Mrs. MacMinnies, "is when we'll be able to get ourselves down that lane and out of here."

"I tried to get somebody to plow you out," Charlie said, "but it seems like every snowplow in the county is tied up. The dairy farms have to get cleared first so's they can get their milk to market. And the town plow isn't allowed to be used on private roads except in cases of emergency."

"If this isn't an emergency, what is?" Mrs. MacMinnies asked, bridling.

Amanda said thoughtfully, "When it's cleared we'll probably have to go back to school."

"Didn't you know?" Charlie said in surprise. "There

hasn't been any school this week. The roads've been too bad, up until today. It probably won't start up again until tomorrow or the day after."

Both Amanda and Obie looked dashed at this. I couldn't help gloating. I was the only one who was really having a holiday, after all.

Charlie rose from his chair. "Well, I'm going now. Tell Mr. Little I'll probably be back on the job tomorrow, if I can get my truck up here." He turned to Mrs. MacMinnies. "Is there anything else you want? I could bring it when I come."

"The only thing I want," she replied, "is out."

Obie said hurriedly, "James and I'll go down to your truck with you."

Charlie appeared dubious. "It's still kind of deep in spots."

"We can go part way, at least," I put in.

Amanda said, "That's a good idea. I'll come too."

"You'll stay right here, Amanda," Obie told her.

"Why should I?" She tossed her head and gave him her beetling Heathcliff look.

"Well," Obie began lamely, "supposing—"

"Supposing what?"

Obie looked rattled. "Look here, Amanda," he said.

Her eyes glinted dangerously. "You're up to something. I know it. I feel it in my bones. And I want to come. I hate being left out of things."

"I want to come too," DeeDee piped up.

That settled the matter so far as Mrs. MacMinnies was concerned.

"Both you girls will stay right here and help me put away all these things." Her mouth was stitched into the grim line beyond which none of us ever dared to go.

Obie breathed a low whistle of relief. He shot Mrs.

MacMinnies a grateful glance, and then we wasted no time in getting out of there with Charlie.

Once we were safely outside, Charlie turned to us. He wasn't grinning any longer.

"All right," he said. "Let's have it. What's up?"

15

WE CAPTURE
A GHOST

I guess our astonishment must have been stamped all over our faces, because Charlie said, "You might just as well spit it out. I know something queer is going on. And you two are mixed up in it."

Obie looked at me. I looked at Obie. Then we both looked at Charlie.

Obie said lamely, "What makes you think?"

Charlie grinned again.

"I was a boy once myself, not too long ago," he said. "What's more, your faces are like glass. I can see right through them."

Over his shoulder Obie glanced at the house. No one was at the windows. "As a matter of fact," he said, his face serious, "something very funny is going on. I thought maybe you might help us." -

"I got to know what it is, first."

"All right," Obie said. He pulled Charlie by the sleeve

around the corner of the house, to the side where we had seen the severed telephone wires. "What do you think of this, Charlie?"

"What do I think of what?"

"Those wires."

We eyed Charlie tensely while he stopped and examined them.

"Cut all right, and neat job, too. How'd it happen?"

"That's what we want you to help us about."

"I can't fix them, if that's what you want," Charlie said. "I wouldn't fiddle with them for anything. The company'll have to come and do that. What did you want to do it for?" His brown eyes were as sorrowful as a Saint Bernard dog's. "It's the wrong kind of mischief for you boys to get into."

I was shocked. "We didn't do it," I said. "We wouldn't think of doing anything so stupid."

His face turned stern. "Well, who did?"

"That's the whole problem, Charlie," Obie said eagerly. "We think we know. But we're going to need your help in nabbing the ghost."

"The ghost? What ghost? Are you loco? Ghosts don't go around cutting telephone wires."

"This ghost did," Obie said.

Charlie said, "Look, I got to get back to my truck. I haven't got time for this kind of fooling around."

"We're not fooling around," I said.

Obie nudged me. "You explain it to him, James," he said. "You can do it better than I could."

Well, I told Charlie as quickly as I could what we hadn't mentioned while he was in the kitchen. I told him how the power went on and off and on again, and about Obie's hunch, and the tracks, and about our going down to the barn and what we saw there. When I finished, Charlie gawked at us both.

"Whew!" he said.

Obie produced the wooden contraptions. "These are what made those tracks, Charlie. I found them by the barn door."

Charlie inspected them carefully.

"Yep," he said, "very interesting. Now, what did you say this phantom of yours looked like?"

Obie nudged me a second time.

"We don't really know," I explained. "We didn't hang around long enough to find out, except that it was a man and he hadn't shaved in a long time, and . . . and that's about it."

Charlie gave his trousers a hitch. "We're going down to the barn now." He stood and thought for a moment. "Maybe I'd better mush down to the truck and get a crowbar, in case there's any violence."

"Would this do?" Obie asked. He pulled something else out of his bulging jacket. It was the carving knife that had been lying on the kitchen table. "I picked it up when Mrs. MacMinnies wasn't watching."

Charlie looked grave. "Maybe you'd better let me have that," he said.

Obie surrendered the knife to him and we started down the lane.

Everything was muffled by the snow: our footsteps, our voices, even our spirits. We were setting off on an adventure, sure enough, but it was a grisly one. We watched the barn as we drew closer to it, but we saw no sign of life there: only the door that we had left open when we made that wild rush out of the place, banging idiotically back and forth as the wind pushed it. We were careful to inspect the ground for footprints. The only tracks we found were those that had been made by Obie and me. I couldn't help feeling relieved that there weren't any new ones.

We were more than halfway to the barn when the dogs came over to us: Maggie bounding and Sieglinde waddling through the snow as fast as she could on those sawed-off legs of hers.

Charlie jerked his gloved thumb in Maggie's direction.

"I see the old girl looks a lot tamer than the last time I was here," he said. "It didn't take long, did it?"

Maggie came up and sniffed at his heels while Sieglinde wriggled shamelessly until he bent over and patted her. Obie and I were sort of astounded that Maggie didn't carry on. "I guess she knows you all right, Charlie," Obie said, impressed.

"Of course she knows I won't hurt her," Charlie said. "And she knows I like dogs." He stroked her muzzle gently. "Maggie's no fool. Never was."

But as soon as we got to the barn door, Maggie began acting up again.

"Be quiet!" I told her. "Go home, Maggie!" After all, we didn't want her warning the ghost of our approach.

Maggie wouldn't leave us, though. She wouldn't leave off barking, either.

"Let her be, James," Charlie told me. "I guess she doesn't care for ghosts any more than we do."

We pushed slowly through the narrow doorway into the barn.

The barn itself was just as we had left it: cold and vast and gloomy. Snow still lay like powder on the floor where it had drifted in. The wind whipped through the place, whistling in a way that was almost human. The door creaked behind us.

The dogs remained outside. Maggie wouldn't venture

any nearer than the radius of the door, and Sieglinde wasn't going anywhere without the collie. I could hear Maggie's desolate high whining. It made an eerie background to our stealthy movements.

"Maybe he won't be there after all," I suggested in a low voice. "Maybe he's gone by now."

"Be quiet, James," Obie flung at me irritably. He said the words between clenched teeth, so I knew that he was as edgy as I was.

Charlie whispered, "I wish I'd had sense enough to bring along a flashlight."

"I have one," Obie whispered back. "Here." And he produced it from the depths of his jacket.

Charlie gave him a nod of approval and took it from him. He flashed the powerful beam around the barn.

There was nothing to be seen: only all that cavernous emptiness, and the trapdoor standing open, precisely as we had left it. The naked electric light bulb was still on, although it made only the feeblest glimmer, so that the place was clogged with thick shadow.

Obie said in a cautious undertone, "Down there is where we saw him."

"Maybe I'd better go first," Charlie said.

Well, that was all right with us.

We watched Charlie's head disappear. Obie followed him. I couldn't help quaking a little as I went down the ladder, rung by rung, in my turn. I wasn't quaking so much as I might have, though. After all, Charlie was there with us. It made a difference.

When I found my footing on the freezing concrete floor, Charlie and Obie were already standing beside those bales of dirty hay. The air was suffocatingly close down there, and the nasty smell made me want to gag.

Charlie flicked on the flashlight.

Our ghost was still there, all right. He hadn't moved from the place. He lay all twisted up, one arm flung out, with his face hidden and resting on the khaki sleeve of an old army jacket. His legs sprawled queerly, like a marionette's. His clothes were stained and crumpled, and they smelled awful.

In a voice that made me start, Charlie said, "Get up!"

The ghost didn't stir. He just lay there, huddled and very still.

Half hopefully, half in fear, I said, "Maybe he's dead." And I gulped.

Charlie grunted and prodded him in the side with the toe of his boot. The ghost stirred slightly then and let out a low moan.

We drew back instinctively. It was as though a rattlesnake had just rattled at us in the straw.

"He's real enough, this ghost of yours," Charlie muttered. "What's more, he's alive." With a sudden movement Charlie seized him by the shoulder and turned him over.

A haggard face, pale under what must have been over a week's growth of dark stubble, winced up at us under trickles of cold sweat on the lean cheeks. The eyes, however, remained closed. If it wasn't a ghost we were looking at, it seemed nearly enough like a dead man's mask to be one.

We stared down at the gaunt features with their blue-shadowed skin. Charlie expelled a deep breath.

"Do you recognize him, Charlie?" I whispered, and Obie looked hopefully at Charlie. "Can you tell who it is?"

Before Charlie could answer, the ghost's lips parted and he began to mumble. It was so faint, that mumbling, as to be almost impossible to hear.

"What's he saying?" Charlie demanded fiercely. "Can you make any of it out? Listen carefully, James. It may be important."

I bent over with my ear close to the man's mouth, and listened. Through the heavy uneven breathing I could just manage to make out a few words. I repeated them as he spoke.

"Where is it?" the voice kept repeating hoarsely. "Where is it?" And then: "The dog has it. . . . That's what she said the last time I saw her. . . . The dog has it! . . . But she was wandering. The old woman was too far gone by then. . . . How could the blasted dog have it?. . . But she said . . ." The words trailed off into something unintelligible. Then he stopped.

I waited, but no more words came.

I looked up at Charlie anxiously.

"Can you figure any of it out?"

He shook his head, frowning. I could see he was perplexed.

He said slowly, "None of it made any sense to me." Then, holding the knife in readiness in one hand, he reached down and grabbed the ghost by one flopping arm and shook him, hard.

The eyes opened, but they were blank. They didn't seem to see, and the dry lips worked without any sound coming from them.

"All right," Charlie said brusquely, "get up!"

The ghost just lay there staring up at us. His eyes looked exactly as though they were made of dull glass.

"Either he's playing a good game of possum," Charlie declared at last, "or else he's sick." He turned to Obie. "Here," he said, handing him the knife, "take this. If he tries anything, which I doubt, go ahead and use it."

Then Charlie knelt and with surprising gentleness touched the ghost's forehead with the back of his hand.

Obie brandished that knife like a commando. "Is he putting on an act?" he asked.

"I guess not. He's got a high fever. Here, James, you turn the flash on him while I do some investigating."

I held the light steadily as I could while Charlie slowly and methodically ran his big hands down the ghost's side and along his legs.

Suddenly he stopped.

"What is it, Charlie?"

"Leg's broken, right at the thigh." He glanced around. "He must of fallen in the barn here and snapped it. Or maybe those stilt things he was going around on weren't fastened tight enough. He could even have taken a freak header into a drift." He considered. "Yep," he went on, "that's what happened. Look: you can see where he must of dragged himself along the floor. Then he crawled back here somehow. How he managed it, beats me." He looked up at us. "And that's about it."

"But why—?"

"Never mind about the whys. We'll have to work all that out later. Right now I have to do what I can for him. He's probably passed out from the pain. Give me that knife."

"What are you going to do now?" Obie asked, his eyes popping.

"I'm going to make a splint. It's the only thing to do. Bring me some strong sticks, one of you."

I scrounged around until I found a couple. When I brought them back, Charlie had already slashed the trouser leg. With the sticks and his own scarf he cradled the broken thigh in a neat splint. "Now we have to make sure he's warm."

There was a heap of stuff against the wall: cans of soup, some dirty plates, a crate with more dirty dishes on it, along with an unwashed saucepan and things like that. A little cook stove on a dresser in a corner. Beyond that there was a bed, strewn with old clothes, tools, and I don't know what. A couple of chairs stood beside the bed. They were piled with dirty laundry. "So that's what happened to the things from the honey house," Charlie said between his teeth. He fossicked about on the bed until he found some ratty old blankets. "No sense moving him," he said, and we covered him with those.

Charlie stepped back and surveyed him. "He ought to have something to kill the pain," he said thoughtfully, "except that he's probably beyond feeling much of anything right now. Is there any whiskey up at the house?"

"I know there isn't," Obie said. "I heard Poppa say so the day of the storm."

"We'll have to forget about it then. Right now I'd better beat it down to the village and see if there's any way of getting Barney out of here and to a doctor."

"Barney!" I exclaimed.

"Barney?" Obie echoed.

"Sure," Charlie said. "That's Barney Rudkin. I wondered what'd happened to him. One of you better get him some water, meanwhile. His lips are cracked."

Obie said, "I'll get some snow."

While Obie was gone I stared down at that empty staring face. Charlie was looking down at him too. There was a curious expression in his sad dark eyes.

"Barney Rudkin!" he said under his breath. "I should have figured we hadn't seen the last of him. He always was as slippery as a new deck of cards."

As he said it I had a strange inkling. I couldn't help

feeling that I knew Barney Rudkin's face from some-where. It was a crazy notion, of course, and I realized that it was. And yet I couldn't stop wondering. I tried to look away but my eyes kept coming back to rest on those features, and all the time something was tickling at the back of my mind. I tried to think, but I couldn't. The smell and the closeness of the place and Barney's peculiar breathing, as though every breath was a struggle, made me feel hemmed in and jumpy. As much as I wanted to, I couldn't concentrate two cents' worth. My own thought was to get out of there as quickly as I could and leave the barn and everything it held as far behind me as possible.

Obie came back at last. It seemed as though he'd been gone a week. He'd scooped up a couple handfuls of snow, and now he knelt and let some of it melt on Barney's burning lips.

After a while Charlie said, "He's had enough for now." He crouched down beside the hay. "Barney," he said. "Can you hear me? Barney!"

Barney's eyes had closed. He lay there moaning to himself.

"He's too far gone to talk," Charlie said with a shrug. "I wish I could get him to say something, though. I'd like to know what Barney was up to, hanging around the place after it was sold."

"Maybe he was just trying to scare us," I ventured. "Maybe he didn't like not being able to stay here anymore."

"There's more to it than that." Charlie rubbed his chin pensively. "Trust Barney. He was after something. Barney always was."

"But what?"

"That's what's bothering me." Charlie got to his feet. "Okay," he said at last. "Let's make tracks."

Obie said, "Do you think we ought to tie him up or something, so he won't get away while we're gone?" He reached into that jacket and pulled out a length of chain. It looked familiar to me, but I couldn't exactly place it.

"Where'd you get that?" I asked.

"It's Sieglinde's leash. I brought it along, just in case. And there's something else." He fished around some more and brought out an object with the glint of steel to it.

"Handcuffs!" Charlie burst out. I could see that he was having a hard time trying not to smile. "You think of everything, don't you?"

Obie said modestly, "Well—"

"Where'd you ever find those?" Charlie wanted to know.

"They're part of a detective set I got for Christmas when I was a kid," Obie told him.

"When you were a kid," Charlie repeated, his mouth sort of twitching. "Well, put them away, and the anchor chain too. We won't need them. He can't get far with that leg. Come on, let's get out of here."

We climbed up the ladder.

The barn seemed airy and light after the stink and fug that we'd left behind. I took a couple of good deep breaths.

Maggie was hovering just outside the door. She bounded forward to greet us, her ears pricked.

Charlie said, "No wonder Maggie made such a racket. She knew he was there all along. She never could stand the sight or smell of Barney."

Obie's jaw clenched. "Do you think Barney mistreated her?"

Charlie shrugged.

"Who knows? Anyway, he didn't take much care of

her. The only one Barney ever thought of was himself. Dogs have a way of sensing things like that."

"Maggie's pretty smart, anyway," Obie said, looking her way sort of proudly.

Then I remembered something.

"'The dog has it'; that's what Barney said. I wonder if that didn't really mean something?"

Charlie considered for a moment. Then, with a swing of his arm, he waved the idea away. "That was just the delirium. Barney didn't know what he was saying. He was only raving. You'd be, too, if you'd been lying there all that time with a bad break in your leg."

"But why was he there?" Obie persisted. "And why did he cut the wires and turn off the current?"

Charlie shrugged again. "We'll find out soon enough, I guess."

Obie said, "I wonder if we ought to tell the others now."

"That's up to you," Charlie answered. "There'll be time enough to tell them the whole story later, when we take him away. Maybe, for now, it'd be smarter to leave it this way. No need getting your folks in a regular uproar. They'd just come down here and make everything worse. It's not as though anybody can do much for him right now and we've already taken care of what had to be done. Let him lie there a little longer. I've seen men a lot worse than he is, and they came out all right."

"Is there anything else we ought to do?" Obie asked.

"You might sneak down and give him some more water after a while. A couple of extra blankets'd help. You might even try giving him some soup. The whole thing is to keep him warm. I'll be back soon as I can, but I can't be sure when that'll be. It'd be crazy trying to move him until we can get your road clear, and I'm not sure how long I'll have to wait to get a plow to come up."

"Right, Charlie," Obie said.

Maybe it was being out in the air again that did it, but I suddenly remembered the Old Man. I mean, he hadn't had any word from me for days, and although there wasn't any need to be, he was probably concerned. I turned to Charlie. "Would you do something for me, Charlie?" I asked.

"Sure," he said. "What?"

"Would you call up the Old Man—my father, that is—and tell him I'm all right? You can call him collect. His name is James Gregory Smith, Senior."

"What's his number?"

It so happened that I had a stub of pencil on me, and an old envelope I'd been saving on account of the stamp. I put down the Old Man's number, at home and at the office. Then I had another idea. I guess it was the cold and the clarity of the air and all that got me to thinking again. I said, "Charlie, would you tell him something else for me? It may sound funny, but he'll understand."

"What's that?"

"I'll write it down." And I did.

Charlie took the envelope, glanced at it, then gave me an odd look. "Well, James, I'll tell him," he said.

He turned to go. Suddenly he stopped.

"Darn it," he exclaimed. "I knew I'd forgotten something."

"What did you forget?"

"The mail. I meant to bring it up with me from the box. Never mind. I'll get it when I come back. You've waited this long, I guess you can wait a little longer." With a wry salute he plunged off through the drifts in his high rubber boots.

Obie and I stood there. The wind blew thinly. We couldn't help shivering a little as we watched Charlie Murofino's lanky figure pick its way down the lane toward the truck, toward the road, toward the world outside Walkaway Hill.

16

STIR-CRAZY

We waited there until he was out of sight. Then we turned and started back toward the house.

The dogs went with us.

As we kicked our way through the powdery drifts I found myself thinking about all the things that had happened so far. The more I thought, the more confused I got. I mean, I kept trying to make sense out of it all, but nothing really fell into place the way it always does at the end of a real detective story.

Obie had been unusually silent, so I knew that he was brooding about it too.

"Well, James?" he said at last.

"Well what?"

"Well anything."

"It's funny, Obie," I said. "Who'd have thought that we'd ever end up in the middle of a real-life mystery?"

He said glumly, "Some mystery."

"It's the only one we've ever been in," I said. "Only now that it's all over it doesn't seem to have amounted to much."

Obie didn't answer. We plodded ahead. Suddenly he stopped and veered around to face me.

"James," he said, "it's a real mystery still. Look here. The whole thing's practically solved, but we really know less about it than we did before. Something's still wrong."

"That," I admitted, "is just what I was thinking."

"I wish we knew more about that Barney Rudkin."

For once I didn't say anything.

"At least this much is clear," Obie went on. "We've found out that it was Barney Rudkin who was hanging around in the barn. I guess it's pretty evident that he must have been living there ever since we moved to Walkaway Hill."

"How could he have done that?"

"Easy. He must have had a store of food laid by, or else he snitched stuff from the house. We never lock up at night." He kicked at a lump of ice. "It's queer, though, that we didn't see him."

"Amanda did," I reminded him.

"Not really," he said. "We weren't sure what it was she saw."

"And Maggie knew he was there," I added.

Obie nodded impatiently. "Never mind about that now. The point is that it must have been Barney Rudkin who cut the wires and fiddled around with the power switch."

I said I thought that was pretty evident too.

"All right so far," Obie said. "But why? What was the point of it all? It doesn't make any sense. No, James, it's a mystery and it's going to stay one until we know what his motive was."

"If we knew that," I said, "I suppose we would know everything and the case would be solved."

"It's all so fishy," Obie went on, disregarding what I'd said. "What did Barney stand to gain? I thought for a while that maybe he was trying to frighten us, to make us leave Walkaway Hill so he could stay on. Still, he must have known we'd flush him out sooner or later."

I agreed.

Obie thought some more.

"Then there were the words he said," he continued. "I can't help feeling they were supposed to mean something."

"You heard Charlie. He said it was only delirium."

Obie pressed his lips into a stubborn, unbelieving line.

"They must have had *some* meaning to them. People don't just talk. I wish we could figure out what he was trying to say."

Standing still out there in the snow only made it colder. I shrugged. "Come on, Obie," I said. "My feet are getting number than a snowman's. Let's go home."

Across the stretch of snow the house loomed, white and placid and gratifyingly solid. The snowman looked kind of battered, but he still wore his grin. Maybe it was because of the way the light fell on it that the grin now seemed a mocking smirk. Or maybe I just imagined it. Anyway, except for that, the big house appeared as cozy as an old-fashioned Christmas card, with its shutters and chimneys and those funny little attic windows and all. I thought of the warm kitchen. I had a sudden vision of Mrs. MacMinnies's full cookie jar. It sort of helped to wipe out the horror of what we'd seen in the barn. I began to walk faster. I would have run, except that you couldn't in the deep snow.

The dogs must have had the same idea. They raced ahead of us, and they were waiting on the porch. Maggie, standing there, looked very noble and aristocratic, and I realized for the first time what a truly handsome creature she was.

Well, the peaceful aspect of the house turned out to be a snare and a delusion. The minute we set foot inside, Obie and I knew that something was wrong.

The first person we saw was DeeDee. She sat on the hall floor with a lot of old magazines spread around her. A pair of scissors hung disregarded in her hand. She looked fretful and sulky, and when she saw us she just didn't say anything.

Then Amanda stalked past us. The greeting she gave us was baleful and perfunctory. It was plain to see that there was no forgiveness in her heart just then.

An ominous silence hung heavily over everything.

And then, like an arrow, a voice twanged through the air. It came from the direction of the kitchen and it belonged to Mrs. MacMinnies.

"I'm going back to the world the minute that lane opens up, please God. And you can tell the mister that for me."

Aunt Claire's voice came next, distressful and remonstrating. "But you can't leave us, Mrs. MacMinnies!"

"I can," came the prickly retort, "and I will. I'm handing in my notice as of this instant."

"Oh, dear, this is dreadful. Whatever in the world will we do without you, Mrs. MacMinnies?"

"Ah you won't even miss me. There's many a foolish old girl will come in my place." The voice softened momentarily. "Mind, it's not you Littles that I'm leaving." Then it hardened again. "It's this terrible cursed life in the country that I can't take any more of. And I'll thank you, Mrs. Little, not to try to make me change my mind. It's made up. I put my foot down this time."

Dire silence fell. Then there was a distinct bang. It wasn't Mrs. MacMinnies's foot, but it might just as well have been. It meant that she had marched up to her room and had let the door slam behind her.

A moment later Aunt Claire appeared in the hall. She was pale and so distraught that she didn't even notice us as she fled up the stairs to Uncle Oliver's study, which made it perfectly clear to us all how serious the putting down of Mrs. MacMinnies's foot had been.

It left the household pretty much in a state of shock. DeeDee pouted. Amanda retreated to some private hiding place, leaving the field to us.

We seized the opportunity at once. We borrowed some blankets from the linen closet. Then we heated up a can of chicken soup and filled a thermos flask with it. We also snitched some cookies for ourselves, but they somehow didn't taste right. Then we streaked back to the barn with the blankets and the soup.

We managed to get some of that soup down Barney's gullet, but most of it dribbled to the floor. We wrapped the blankets around him as best we could. And that was all we could do, so we beat it back to the house.

As we crept into the hall we heard Uncle Oliver's ringing voice. It clanged down from his study.

"She's stir-crazy, Claire. I tell you, that's the whole trouble," he stated. "But she's not the only one. You're stir-crazy. I'm stir-crazy. The children are stir-crazy. We're all stir-crazy, for the love of Pete. It's this confounded snow. We've all had a sight too much of it." We could hear his hand slam the desk. "I wish Whittier were alive so I could stuff some of it down his throat, along with a copy of his infernal *Snow-bound*."

After that everyone was more or less on edge, for different reasons.

Uncle Oliver, once he had been interrupted in his daily session with Hal Sterling, found that he couldn't go back to it. He prowled around the house like a riled bear, rumpled and gruff. Aunt Claire fluttered about in the kitchen, trying to appease Mrs. MacMinnies, who had finally emerged from seclusion and went about her duties, glowering as though she were some discontented monument. Aunt Claire's nervous efforts only made her more adamant about going back to live with her married cousin in Brooklyn Heights. Amanda was being especially irritating, acting snooty and pretending not to notice me or Obie because we wouldn't let her in on the secret she was certain we had between us. As a matter of fact, we had thought seriously of telling her. But now that she had made up her mind to be haughty, we were determined not to tell her after all, not until the last minute. So she went off sulking somewhere again. And DeeDee was even more fretful than before because nobody would pay any attention to her, not even the dogs who lay snoozing on top of the hot-air registers.

As for Obie and myself, we had enough to be edgy about, what with watching the lane and waiting for Charlie.

After half an hour or so passed without any sign of him, or of the men to fix the telephone, or a snowplow or an ambulance or anything, we stole down to the barn again. This time we took Barney some hot tea, and, in case he was hungry, a couple of liverwurst sandwiches.

Nothing in the barn had changed. He still lay there, sort of half conscious. He wasn't even mumbling. Secretly we hoped he might say something that would be an important clue. He swallowed some tea, but he wouldn't eat. I ended up with both sandwiches myself.

Then we stood in the lane, out of sight of the house, watching for Charlie until it finally got too dark to see anything.

We trudged dispiritedly back.

We got a start as we came near the house. Out of the gloom something white emerged. It seemed to be coming toward us. We dove into the nearest snowdrift. Then we saw that it was only old Abominable, but it just goes to show you how truly on edge we were by then.

Things hadn't improved much in the house, either.

Supper was grim.

When it was over, everyone sort of scattered. There wasn't going to be any cozy sitting around the fire. Aunt Claire and Uncle Oliver went upstairs to frame the terms of the possible peace treaty they hoped to make with Mrs. MacMinnies. Amanda, haughtier than ever, because of something Obie had said, which I won't bother to repeat, vanished up the staircase with the *Collected Poems* of Edna St. Vincent Millay under her arm. Unfortunately for her, I had already spotted the gaudy cover of one of Uncle Oliver's paperback thrillers sticking out of the back pocket of her blue jeans, so that spoiled the dignity of her exit. Mrs. MacMinnies, majestic and still prickly, remained in possession of the kitchen. She sat in her rocker, knitting like Madame Defarge and grimly listening to the radio. And DeeDee was fooling around somewhere with Maggie and Sieglinde.

I turned to Obie.

"Well?" I said.

He made a face like a gargoyle's at me.

"What can we do, Obie? It's still early."

"I don't know about you," he said shortly, "but I'm going up to my room. I want to think in peace."

In the end I went with him. I said that it was because his room faced out toward the lane and the barn, and we could sit at the window. I have to admit that this wasn't entirely true. It was only part of the truth. The real reason was that, considering everything that had happened, I didn't feel like staying by myself.

Anyway, up there we would be the first to see any headlamps or flashlights that came up Walkaway Hill. Frankly, I no longer expected anyone to arrive that night, but I kept on hoping. I was especially anxious to have the telephone repairmen show up because I was eager to hear from the Old Man.

Nothing happened. I stared out at all that snow. It seemed incredible that there could be so much of it in one place. It was a white night, too, and the moon made everything a lot brighter. The wind had died down. Not even the branches rattled outside the window. I figured then that it wouldn't be until sometime in the morning that Charlie would return with the plow to open up the lane.

The stillness was appalling.

"Obie," I said at last.

"What?"

"I can't just sit and think."

"Then just sit."

I tried, but it didn't work.

From outside, in the hall, I could hear DeeDee babbling to the dogs, and a lot of thumping, which meant that she was dressing them up in those absurd get-ups she'd made for them. Fainter still came the voices of Aunt Claire and Uncle Oliver, deep in domestic discussion, and, from what seemed miles away, the drone of Mrs. MacMinnies's radio.

I got up.

"Obie, I've got to do something," I told him. "I'm getting jittery."

He threw me an impatient glance, like Einstein disturbed in the middle of solving the problem of relativity. "What's there to do until Charlie arrives?"

"I don't know," I confessed. "But I want to do it anyway."

Just then I heard a small furtive sound, no louder than the scrabbling of a mouse's paws, at Obie's door.

Obie leaped up off his stool.

"James," he whispered in alarm, "did you hear that?"

The scrabbling sound came again, louder this time.

Cautiously, Obie went to the door. He hesitated for a moment.

"Go ahead," I whispered. "Open it."

He took a breath. Then he opened it.

"Oh," I heard him say. "It's you."

It was Amanda.

17

THE OTHER MAGGIE

"**W**hat," Obie demanded churlishly, "do you want?"

Amanda shifted her weight from one foot to the other. She scuffed a moccasin along the floor and peered at us. She didn't look stormy and intense anymore. She just seemed rather forlorn. Obie and I had both seen that lily maid of Astolat expression before, however.

She said, lamely, at last, "What in the world were you two doing, sitting here in the dark?"

"It's not so dark," I answered. "There's all that moonlight."

She edged a step forward.

"Would you mind if I came in, Obie?"

"It's a free country," he told her.

She still appeared hesitant.

"Are you coming in or not?" Obie said.

"Look here, Obie," Amanda burst out abruptly, "I

simply hate doing things without you and James. And everything's so absolutely loathsome anyway. I can't bear it. I'll say Pax if you will."

Obie and I glanced at each other. Then we couldn't help smiling, not so much in triumph but because we'd known Amanda wouldn't hold out. She never can hang on to a sulking fit for long.

"Sure, Amanda," Obie said. "Pax." He held up his right hand.

"Pax," I said, doing likewise.

And armistice it was.

We all heaved sighs of relief and Amanda settled herself on the bed, cross-legged like an Indian yogi.

"I'm glad that's settled," she said chattily. "Now I wish you'd tell me your secret. Please, Obie."

"I thought there'd be something like that," he snorted.

"You don't have to tell me if you don't really want to," she replied humbly. But her eyes were still pleading.

"We'll tell you as soon as we possibly can, Amanda," I promised. I was reluctant to spoil the Pax so soon.

"Eventually, why not now?"

"We just can't," Obie put in. "You wouldn't sleep a wink tonight if we did."

That only made it worse. Amanda's eyes got even larger and more avid than before.

I was all for telling her then, but Obie wouldn't give in. "Amanda's such a chatterbox. She'd spill it to everyone else, right away."

"Not this time. I swear on my sacred oath I wouldn't."

But Obie remained inflexible. He can be pretty stubborn at times. The secret was more Obie's than mine, in a way, so although Amanda turned those pleading orbs on me, I couldn't go against his decision.

Amanda said at length, "So that's the way it is?"

"That's the way it's going to stay," Obie answered.

"Well, thanks a bunch." Then Amanda began to whistle "Greensleeves" off-key to show that she didn't really care anyway.

Suddenly she stopped whistling, right in the middle of a phrase.

"Listen, you two," she said. "I have an idea."

Obie grimaced. "Not Wuthering Heights again!"

Amanda refused to be put off.

"We can't just lurk here in the dark, doing nothing," she retorted.

Obie glanced uneasily out of the window. There was still no sign of anything approaching from the outside world. There was only poor chilly Abominable, keeping his ghostly vigil on the lawn.

"What's up your shifty raveled sleeve this time?"

Amanda looked sibylline.

"We could explore," she said.

"Explore? At this time of night?"

"Why not?"

"What's there left to explore? We've seen everything."

"Not quite everything," Amanda rejoined. Her Mona Lisa smile was exasperatingly mysterious.

"All right," Obie challenged. "What's left?"

"There's the attic, for one thing." She sounded very casual as she said it.

But she knew she had scored. It was true. The attic was the one place we'd forgotten to go through.

I could tell at once that Obie was tempted. He was also loath to leave the window. As for me, I was wild to see what the place was like.

I went up to him. "Come on, Obie," I said in his ear. "Charlie won't come any more today. And if he does, we'll still see his lights from the windows in the attic. You couldn't miss them from up there."

That clinched it.

"All right," he conceded. "We might as well find out what's up there. There probably won't be anything more exciting than a lot of dust." He stretched. "Still and all, it won't hurt to have a quick look around."

Amanda's face was bright and eager again.

"You never can tell," she said, getting all breathless. "We might discover something really marvelous: a trunk brimming with ancient doubloons, or crumbling old maps showing where the hidden treasure of Walkaway Hill is buried, or—or anything!"

I couldn't help catching some of Amanda's excitement. It always happens to me. Things never stay quite ordinary around Amanda.

Obie cast a look of unspeakable contempt at both of us.

"You and your books!" he told Amanda. He stretched again. "Well, if we're going exploring, I'd better trot downstairs and get a flashlight first."

"That's what I love about my brother Obie," Amanda pronounced with a smile. "He's always so practical."

"Somebody has to be practical in this crowd," he flung back at her as he disappeared.

He was back in a flash with the flashlight. We filed out into the hall and along its length to the place just outside Uncle Oliver's studio where the attic trapdoor was. Obie yanked at the dangling cord. The wooden frame swung downward, revealing the steps that lay nested against it. He unhooked them. They reached to the floor. Above our heads gaped a black rectangular hole.

"I'll go first," Obie announced. " I have the flashlight."

He was about to start up the stairs when, as though from nowhere, DeeDee appeared. She was dragging

Maggie and Sieglinde behind her by two lengths of tangled rope. Their paws click-clacked reluctantly against the wooden boards. They trailed odd bits of finery and their wake was littered with the ribbons and oddments they had shaken off on the way.

Obie groaned.

"Who invited you, DeeDee?"

"I'm tired of playing all by myself," she informed him. "I want to go with you and Amanda and James."

"You have Maggie and Sieglinde. Aren't they enough?"

"They won't stay dressed up," DeeDee complained. "And anyhow, I want to go where you're going."

"It's dark up there," he warned, "and spidery."

"I don't care."

"I know what. You could stay down here and be our lookout," he suggested craftily.

DeeDee refused to be taken in. "You're going exploring. I heard you planning it in your room, and I want to go with you."

"It's not exactly the Lewis and Clark Expedition. We're only going up to the attic to poke around."

"Well, I want to poke around too."

"You'll get your clothes dirty."

DeeDee's dimpled chin turned to steel. "If you don't let me come," she threatened, "I'll tell Poppa."

"Oh, let her come," said Amanda. "It'll be less trouble that way. We'll never hear the end of it if we leave her behind."

"And I want Sieglinde and Maggie to come too!"

It was useless remonstrating with her. DeeDee may be the smallest, but she is also the stubbornest of the Littles. So along she came. I was the last to go because I had to give the dogs a boost. They refused to go up the folding stairs by themselves.

Once we were there it took a while to get our bearings. Obie fiddled around with his usual efficiency until he found a light. It wasn't very strong. Still, we could see right away that there wasn't much up there, except for the dry smell of dust and neglect that places have when they've been unused for a long time. There were also a lot of sleepy hornets that droned resentfully at being disturbed. Sieglinde plumped down on her backside near the edge of the trapdoor and wouldn't budge, but Maggie started snuffling in the far corners.

Obie turned to DeeDee. "She's probably going after bats and mice and stuff. Are you sure you still want to stick around?

DeeDee tossed her head. "I'm not afraid of bats and mice. I'd make a house for them and have them for pets."

Obie shrugged. "Okay," he said. "But don't say I didn't warn you."

We all started poking around in the dimness. Obie had the advantage because he had the flashlight. He was the first one to uncover something.

"Hey, see what I found!" he trumpeted.

Amanda and I dashed over to inspect his trophy.

"It's nothing but an old croquet set," Amanda said, but I could tell that she was miffed at not having bagged it first.

Then Amanda fished a mirror from a pile of old frames, only it was broken.

"That means seven years bad luck," Obie told her, gloating.

"Not to me. I didn't break it."

There were lots of dusty cartons, but all we could discover in them were old dresses that crumbled to bits as we hauled them out, and broken Christmas tree ornaments, and a teapot with its spout missing, and hundreds—well, dozens—of empty candy boxes. It looked as though Mrs. Houghton had never thrown anything out, ever.

"That's about it," I said in disappointment. "No doubloons, no maps, no treasure."

Obie nodded. "We might as well go back down. You can carry the croquet set, James."

"We can't play croquet in the snow," I said. "Besides, it's awfully heavy."

"Take it anyway," he commanded. He looked around. "Where's Maggie?"

We couldn't see her.

We staggered around, stumbling over all that junk, searching for her. Finally Obie flashed a beam of light into a far corner. It was the one place none of us had bothered to investigate. Because of the way the house was built it was easy to overlook: the angle of the roof hid it as effectively as if it had been walled off. No one would have seen it if Maggie hadn't sniffed it out.

"Hey!" Obie shouted. "Take a look at this, will you?"

In the murky light I could just about distinguish a group of strange, spectral shapes.

For a moment I thought I was looking at a small cemetery. There was a lumpy angel with one drooping wing bending over what seemed to be the pallid head of a child. Another angelic figure hovered nearby with its white arms folded across its breast. A large and naked foot that didn't seem to belong to anything suddenly emerged from the dusty gloom. A white cat crouched, immobile, beside it.

I gasped.

"I want to go downstairs now," DeeDee wailed.

Obie advanced with the flashlight. I followed, keeping a safe distance behind him.

Nothing stirred.

Everything remained rigid, huddling there like so many spider-webbed statues.

And suddenly I realized that they were exactly that: statues. It was as though we had stumbled onto a forgotten corner of some museum.

"They must be some of Mrs. Houghton's!" I exclaimed. "The Estate didn't find them because they were stuck away here."

"Of course!" Amanda cried. She added, after a moment, "They aren't terribly good, are they?"

And then we caught sight of Maggie. Or, rather, we saw two Maggies staring at each other. It was as though she were confronting herself in a dusty looking-glass. There she squatted, facing her exact duplicate and whining softly, trying to coax her other self to reply. Then she sniffed in a bewildered sort of way. She reached out one paw to touch the sculptured collie. She seemed surprised and puzzled when there was no response. She cocked her head to one side. Then she pointed her muzzle at the ceiling and whined again, deep in her throat.

DeeDee stopped wailing. "I want to see!" she cried.

When we examined the figure it turned out to be half as tall as Maggie herself, and made of some hard tawny stuff. Amanda said it was terra-cotta, and we thought she was just showing off, but later we discovered that she was right. Anyway, it was as like Maggie as though it were her twin.

"I think it's great!" Obie said, marveling.

As a matter of fact, it seemed a lot more expert and alive than any of the other figures in Mrs. Houghton's little graveyard. It wasn't lumpy like the angels, or amateurish-looking like the child's bust or the cat. It had been made with real love and care, with Maggie as its live model, and it looked as though at any moment it might raise its head and bark.

"I think we ought to take it downstairs," Obie said.

Amanda said hopefully, "Maybe we can keep it. It would be sort of a monument to Mrs. Houghton. After all, Walkaway Hill was hers for so long. I'd like to think that after we're gone there'll be something here to remind people of us."

"Oh, Amanda," Obie said, "don't be so morbid."

Amanda seemed surprised. "I'm not being morbid. It's the way I feel." She drew herself up. "Every artist is entitled to some immortality," she said.

So for the time being we forgot about the croquet set. Very carefully I carried the other Maggie down the steps. It was a lot lighter than it looked, I'm glad to say. The real Maggie followed, sniffing eagerly and wagging her tail in delight and puzzlement.

Maggie and I were the last ones down.

There was a reception committee at the foot of the folding steps. It consisted of Uncle Oliver and Aunt Claire.

"What," Uncle Oliver demanded, "is going on here?"

"We were only exploring the attic, Poppa," Amanda said.

"It sounded more like the Thundering Herd over our heads than a party of exploration," he remarked. "And what, James, is that grimy object to which you are clinging?"

"It's a statue, Poppa," Obie said. "We found it up there. Can we keep it, Poppa?"

"Maggie found it, really," amended Amanda.

"Set it down first, James, and let's have a good look at it."

Aunt Claire said, "I think I ought to get a dustrag."

I set it on the floor as gently as I could.

As I did so, the head rolled off.

"Oh, James!" Amanda wailed. "You've broken it. How could you be so clumsy?"

"I didn't break it. Anyway, I didn't mean to."

"You did so break it!" DeeDee cried.

Obie said sarcastically, "I suppose it just came off by itself."

"That's exactly what happened," I said. "It did come off by itself."

"That's enough out of the lot of you," Uncle Oliver broke in. "Recrimination never mended anything. Obie, where's the glue? Maybe I can fix it."

Obie returned with the glue just as Aunt Claire made her reappearance with a dustrag.

Uncle Oliver retrieved the head and began fiddling with it, setting it back where it had been originally.

"That's odd," he said. "It doesn't seem to be broken at all. I mean, it looks as though it was made to come off." He removed the head again. "See what I mean?" He replaced it in order to demonstrate. "Look at that. The edges are perfectly even and the head just fits inside."

This time, however, the head didn't seem to fit. It came off once more.

"I think something's probably obstructing it," Uncle Oliver said, and ran his fingers around the rim of the body part. Suddenly his hand stopped moving. "And what might this be?" he inquired as he drew something out.

We all craned forward to see what it could be.

"It's only a sheet of paper," Obie said.

Uncle Oliver unfolded it slowly.

"What in the world is it, Oliver?" Aunt Claire said.

Obie said, "Mrs. Houghton probably used it for stuffing. Here's the glue, Poppa."

"I doubt very much if stuffing was used in this instance," Uncle Oliver said. "It's a work of art, not a Thanksgiving turkey, Obie." He put on his horn-rimmed glasses. "It looks like a legal document of some sort."

"Really, Oliver," said Aunt Claire. "What would a legal document be doing in there?"

"As a matter of fact," he said, "it bears every appearance of being a last will and testament."

We all gaped at him.

And then everything came over me like a thunderclap.

"That's what he meant all the time, Obie!" I blurted out. "He wasn't raving. The dog had it after all!"

18

SIEGLINDE FINDS HERSELF

The eyes of the entire Little family were upon me. It was very unsettling.

The deathly hush was broken by Uncle Oliver. "What did you mean by that, James?" he inquired.

I threw Obie a stricken look. He was no help. He seemed never to have seen me in his life before. I swallowed once or twice. No words came.

Uncle Oliver cleared his throat. "As the captain of the S.S. *Titanic* remarked when it struck the iceberg, there is considerably more beneath the surface than we suspected." He fixed me with a craggy expression.

I squared my shoulders. "It's a long story, Uncle Oliver," I replied. I sounded sort of lame, but I couldn't help that.

"I thought it might be," he observed as he tucked the document carefully away into his breast pocket. "I think

— 191 —

we had better proceed downstairs at once and hear what James has to tell us."

Uncle Oliver headed the procession. Obie followed with both parts of the terra-cotta collie cradled in his arms. I went last, not only because I didn't feel like facing Amanda's reproachful gaze, but also because I wanted time to think about the best way to tell everything.

I thought all the way down those stairs, even though I knew it was too late to tell anything but the absolute unadorned truth. It seemed sort of foolish, at that point, that Obie and I hadn't let the others in on the secret earlier. It was really Obie's fault, and I was left holding the bag. Anyway, the die was cast. The only trouble was that you can never be sure how so-called grown-ups are going to react to a given situation. Even comparatively enlightened adults like Uncle Oliver and Aunt Claire can be exasperatingly unpredictable at times.

We gathered in the kitchen.

Mrs. MacMinnies, at the sight of us, snapped off her radio and braced herself against the back of her rocker.

"Don't you come bringing any of your delegations in here to me," she declared. "No matter what you say, Mr. Little, I won't be persuaded. I'm leaving the minute that lane is opened, and that's my final word on the subject. His Holiness himself couldn't change my mind, not even if he was to fly all the way from Rome to do it."

Uncle Oliver assured her that the present matter at hand was in no wise concerned with the problem of her departure.

I thought I detected a shadow of disappointment cross her features.

"Then to what do I owe the honor of this visitation?"

she countered. Her glance lit upon the sculpture. "What, Master Obie, is that dirty object you're carrying?"

"It's not an object," replied Amanda coolly. "If you must know, it's a work of art."

She gasped. "It's a what?"

Aunt Claire interrupted hastily. "It's a sculpture, Mrs. MacMinnies. The children found it in the attic."

"Maggie found it, actually," DeeDee put in.

Mrs. MacMinnies raised one eyebrow and sniffed.

"Couldn't you find anything dirtier to drag down here into my kitchen?"

Uncle Oliver held up one hand.

"Enough!" he said. He turned to me. "The floor is yours, James. We are all listening."

Well, that was it. Zero hour had come. So I stopped thinking and told the entire story, right from the beginning. I did my best to tell it as succinctly and clearly as I could. I stumbled over one or two places in the narrative, but on the whole I think I acquitted myself fairly well. From the first sentence right up to the very last word, I had them all pop-eyed.

There was a long silence when I finished. You could have heard a pin drop. In fact, several of Mrs. MacMinnies's hairpins did just that.

"To think that all that was going on under our noses!" she breathed. She was obviously jolted. "As my old Gran used to say, 'It's what you don't know that's always the worst of it.'"

"But that poor man!" Aunt Claire burst out. "How could you have left him there like that? It's positively inhuman! In this day and age, too!"

Uncle Oliver had already gotten to his feet. "We'll have to see what can be done about him at once," he said gravely.

"I'll get a hot-water bottle," Mrs. MacMinnies said.

"There's nothing to do," Obie insisted. "We covered him up, and we went back twice to feed him soup and hot tea. We did everything Charlie told us to."

"I'm sure that wasn't enough," Aunt Claire said, clasping her hands. "I don't care who he is or what he's done, he's sick and we have to look after him. Oliver, I'm going with you. Where's my thermometer?"

"You'll do nothing of the sort," he said. "I'm going by myself."

"Then at least take the boys with you."

"Nonsense."

"But, Oliver—"

"I'm going down there alone, Claire," he said with finality.

We watched at the window until he returned.

"Well, Oliver?" Aunt Claire asked, her face lined with concern.

He stamped the snow from his galoshes.

"The boys were right," he conceded. "There's nothing more we can do. The poor devil's warm, anyway. We'll just have to wait until Mr. Murofino can get up here with a doctor."

"But we really ought to bring him up here!"

"How?"

"On—on a sled!"

He shook his head. "We'd better leave him there, Claire. He's not too badly off, and in a case like this it's best not to move him any more than is absolutely necessary. And besides, there isn't any sled."

"Oh," Aunt Claire said. She bit her lips.

He patted her arm. "It'll be all right, Claire. Worrying won't help him. The boys did pretty well, considering." He removed his galoshes, cap, muffler, overcoat, and all.

"And now," he said, "I think we had better discuss James's story."

Everybody started jabbering at once.

The air was alive with speculation. It was dizzying.

DeeDee was the one who, in the middle of it all, had sense enough to turn to Uncle Oliver.

"Poppa," she said, "you never told us what it is that the dog had."

Uncle Oliver blinked. "That's true," he said.

We clustered around him while he removed the sheet of thick paper from his breast pocket. He put on his spectacles and slowly read it over to himself. We searched his features for a clue as to what it might be about. For the moment, however, Uncle Oliver was being the Great Stone Face.

He read it all over again.

"Goodness, Oliver, what is it?" Aunt Claire said.

He looked sort of bewildered as he thrust the paper into her hand. "Read that, Claire, and see what you can make of it."

Aunt Claire's forehead wrinkled as she skimmed over the document. When she had finished she looked up at him. Her expression was, to say the least, rather peculiar.

"Oliver, what in the world does this mean?"

"'Struth, woman," he exploded. "Can't you read a few lines of script?"

"Oliver, that's no way to talk to me in front of the— Well, really!"

"But don't you understand what it says?"

"I think I do, but I simply can't bring myself around to believing it."

This was too much for the rest of us. I mean, a person can stand just so much shilly-shallying.

"What does it say?" we clamored.

Uncle Oliver coughed portentously.

"This document," he began, "is a will. If it is valid, and there is no reason to think it isn't, since it has been witnessed and signed by two people—of course, we'll have to consult a lawyer to learn if it is really watertight—"

"Poppa," groaned Amanda, "can't you tell us what it's about without all the hems and haws and ifs and ands? Please!"

"Very well," he said briskly. "Here it is. Walkaway Hill now belongs to us."

"Naturally it does," Obie said. "You bought it, didn't you?"

"If you weren't so impatient and didn't keep interrupting, I could explain this to everyone's satisfaction. We've bought Walkaway Hill, quite right. That is, we've made a down payment, and if we keep up the installments on the mortgage for twenty years the place will eventually be ours."

"Well?" Obie said, chafing.

"That, at any rate, was how matters stood until we—I mean Maggie—found this document. This document," he went on solemnly, "is Mrs. Houghton's last will and testament. And in it she left Walkaway Hill to us."

Amanda echoed, incredulous, "To us?"

"That's impossible," Obie stated flatly. "Why, Mrs. Houghton never met us. She didn't even know we existed."

Mrs. MacMinnies directed a remark toward the ceiling to the effect that we had all gone mental from too much snow. "Snow-crazy, that's what they are," she said.

"If you'd all listen for a minute," Uncle Oliver said, "I might elaborate."

We listened.

It seemed, in short, that Mrs. Houghton had bequeathed the entire property known as Walkaway Hill, the house, the outbuildings and all the land, to whosoever would undertake in all responsibility to keep it up in order to maintain her beloved collie and companion, Maggie, in her old home. "And that," concluded Uncle Oliver, "would be us, since we were the ones who took Maggie in."

"Or rather," Amanda amended gravely, "Maggie is the one who took us in. Walkaway Hill is hers, and we're really her guests."

"I suppose you might put it that way," Uncle Oliver said. "It all seems incredible enough to be true."

"Are you positive it's legal, Oliver?" Aunt Claire asked, still looking dubious.

"Why not? It's signed and witnessed by two people. Here are their signatures: Emma Van Sicklen and Harold Van Sicklen."

"I know who they were," Amanda put in. "They worked for Mrs. Houghton. Charlie Murofino told us about them."

Aunt Claire continued to look thoughtful.

"Then why didn't they come forward when she died and say they'd witnessed her will? The lawyers said they couldn't find one anywhere."

"That's simple, Claire. They witnessed Mrs. Houghton's signature, but they didn't necessarily know what the nature of that document was."

"Oh. Well, there's another thing. If Maggie was so important to Mrs. Houghton, why didn't she make sure the will was left with responsible people, like the lawyers? She must have known something might go wrong if she didn't."

"Judging by what I've heard from the lawyers and from other people I've talked to," Uncle Oliver said, "she was a rather secretive and difficult woman. She didn't seem to trust anyone, least of all her lawyers. People have been known to do odder things about their wills, for that matter."

"Then it's all likely to be true!"

"More than likely," he said quietly.

It took a little while for all that to sink in. And Maggie watched us, her tail wagging slowly from side to side, as though she really was aware of what was going on.

Suddenly Obie began whooping and hollering. "Three cheers for Maggie!" he shouted. The rest of us joined in. Maggie, however, didn't seem to care for this demonstration at all. She beat a dignified retreat to the sitting room rug, looking rather like a distinguished elderly lady who had thought she was at a Philharmonic symphony concert, but had found herself, through some error, at an undergraduate football game.

And then the conjectures started all over again.

"I'll bet that's why Barney Rudkin was hanging around the place," Obie said. "He was hunting for that will all the time."

Amanda shook her head. "No, Obie," she said. "He couldn't have been searching for the will."

"Why not?"

"Because Maggie never liked him, and according to Charlie Murofino, he never cared much for her. He didn't even take care of her properly. No, I'm sure Barney Rudkin was after something else."

"What, for heaven's sake?"

Amanda frowned. Then she said with a sudden inspiration, "I know. It was money!"

"What money?" Uncle Oliver demanded.

"The money Mrs. Houghton was supposed to have left somewhere," Amanda explained. "Charlie told us that everyone in the village believed she had a trunkful or something. Charlie says it was just talk. But when she was dying and told Barney Rudkin that the dog had it, he must have thought she meant the money, but all the while she was really trying to tell him where the will was."

"Then why," Obie demanded, "did Barney cut the telephone and turn off the electricity? Was he trying to drive us away? Where could we go during the storm? And how could he expect to go on living here after we came? It doesn't figure."

"Yes, it does," Amanda put in fiercely. "The trouble with you, Obie, is that you have no imagination, and if you'd let me in on it from the beginning, I could have told you."

"Okay, tell me now," he challenged.

She paused for a moment. Then she said, "You see, the way I see it is this. Barney Rudkin kept hoping to find the money all the time, even after we moved in. I think he must have thought he'd get his hands on it any minute, so long as he kept out of sight. And that plan worked, until the day I saw him. He didn't know that you'd convince me that it was just my imagination. And then when we saw him again through the window, he must have panicked and been afraid we'd call in help from the outside. That's why he cut the wires and turned off the power: so that he could stay around at least until the storm was over." She took a breath. "Anyway," she said, "that's my conjecture."

And that, as we found out later, was the true conjecture. Which just goes to show that it was foolish of us to have reckoned without Amanda to begin with.

Uncle Oliver still looked like a man who had been struck by a solid-gold hammer.

Aunt Claire reached out and squeezed his hand. "I still can't believe the place is really ours. Oliver, am I dreaming or is it true?"

"I think so," he said gravely. "Of course, we might never have found the will."

Amanda said, "But we didn't find it. Maggie did. We owe everything to her."

We all stood hushed. Of course it was perfectly true. It was as though Walkaway Hill were Maggie's gift to the Littles, as though she had found the will because she wanted them to have it.

Uncle Oliver was nonplussed. "It's all too much for me," he said. "This is the sort of thing that only happens in books. If anyone offered me the plot on a silver platter I'd say it was all too improbable for my readers to swallow."

"And yet," Aunt Claire said softly, "it happened, and to us."

"Well," he said, "it's about time we had something that Hal Sterling didn't give us."

Obie grinned slyly. "How about renaming the place Shaggy Dog Hill?"

Suddenly we all felt bushed. So much had happened in such a short time that we were beginning to feel it.

Uncle Oliver said, "I suggest we have some cocoa and then go to bed. We can confront this situation in the morning. There's nothing more we can do about it now, anyway. And there's a terrific draft in here."

The door to the woodshed stood ajar. We figured the catch had come loose. I went and closed it.

Mrs. MacMinnies soon had a pot of hot cocoa and a plate of cookies ready. We sat around the table, still finding it hard to think that it was all true. And yet there was the will in Mrs. Houghton's old-fashioned handwriting, right there to prove it. And since Maggie refused to come in and be thanked, Uncle Oliver himself went into the sitting room with a handful of cookies. He bent his knee as he offered them to her. "And as soon as the lane's open," he said, "I'm going to buy the biggest T-bone steak I can find, all for you, Maggie."

Suddenly DeeDee said, "Where's Sieglinde?"

"She was underfoot a moment ago," Mrs. MacMinnies said.

"Well, she's not here now."

"Maybe she's out there with Maggie."

But she wasn't. In fact, she wasn't anywhere to be seen.

Tired as we were, we all had to go searching for her. We tried every room in the house. We even went back up into the attic. Sieglinde seemed to have vanished into thin air.

"Sieglinde!" we called all over the place.

There was no response.

"She'll be back, squirming like a beggar the minute she gets wind of the cookies," Mrs. MacMinnies assured us.

DeeDee was close to tears. As for the rest of us, we were exasperated.

"If you ask me," Obie said, "she just couldn't stand Maggie's getting all the attention."

Then, on a crazy hunch, I opened the door of the woodshed.

The next thing anyone knew, Mrs. MacMinnies had let out a shrill, shattering shriek. As Uncle Oliver remarked later, she seemed instantaneously to have gone right off her rocker, in every sense of the words.

Through the shed door Sieglinde advanced proudly,

her whip of a tail flailing, her head held high and a strange new light in her eyes. I suddenly realized how much slimmer she had grown in the past days. But that wasn't all. From her jaws dangled a very large and very dead rat.

She went straight to Mrs. MacMinnies and dropped it gently at her feet.

I can't say that Mrs. MacMinnies fainted, exactly, but she came pretty close.

Sieglinde, however, paid no attention to what was going on around her. She even ignored Maggie, who came trotting in at that moment. She simply marched, head high, out to the WELCOME mat in the hall and flopped down in the center of it. She heaved a deep sigh, let her muzzle fall onto one forepaw, and closed her eyes. It was as though she no longer needed anyone, not even Maggie.

But we knew that Sieglinde's finding herself was as much Maggie's doing as our finding the will.

19

AND SO WE SAY FAREWELL, ETC.

It was a strange sound that woke me the next morning.

It didn't sound like anything I'd heard at Walkaway Hill in all the time I'd been there. It was a curious, irregular pattering, not spooky at all, but insistent and reassuring. And although it was still early, my bedroom was as bright as a boxful of yellow sunlight.

I lay there in bed trying to decide what the new sound was. It couldn't be twigs pecking against the panes, or the rattle of dry leaves. It wasn't any human noise, either. Yet it went on and on, the rhythm changing from fast to slow and back to fast again. I wondered if it mightn't be that something had sprung a leak, or if it was the bathtub running over.

It grew to be too much for me. I leaped out of bed and dashed into the bathroom. Everything was in order: all the faucets turned tight and the tub empty.

I padded over to the window.

I had to rub my eyes.

The sun was just like a huge billion-watt electric bulb hanging right over the hills, and the whole world had a moist fresh sparkle to it. The air was warm and very still.

Then I knew.

What I had been listening to was the snow, dropping from the eaves of the house as it melted all along the roof. The drip-drip was a kind of happy music everywhere. You couldn't help feeling cheerful, just hearing it.

As I stood, listening, I remembered all the incredible things that had happened the day before: the phantom in the barn, the dog in the attic, the document inside the dog, everything. I remembered, too, that Barney Rudkin would still be lying, feverish, on that dirty straw out in the barn; and that Charlie Murofino ought to be on his way soon, at last. I couldn't help feeling a shivery wave of expectation right down to the small of my back because Charlie would already have spoken on the telephone to the Old Man. He would probably be bringing with him the answer to my all-important question.

I can't recall when I ever got into my clothes more speedily.

I expected to be the first one down, but the dogs had already been let out, which meant that Mrs. MacMinnies was there in the kitchen ahead of me.

The kitchen was so warm, it was practically steaming. Breakfast was set out on the table, and Mrs. MacMinnies sat in her rocker, waiting. She wore what she called her decent clothes, and she had on her good black cloth coat, and a hat with a purple feather. In a row on the floor stood her rubbers, her bulging Gladstone bag with her umbrella tucked under the straps, her portable radio done up in a neat brown paper parcel, and her crownof-thorns plant all swaddled in cotton and settled into a Gimbel's shopping bag.

I said, "Good morning, Mrs. MacMinnies."

In a cathedral voice she wished me a good morning back. She didn't sound as though she really meant it: the good morning, I mean.

I went to the window. The Abominable Snowman didn't look a bit abominable anymore. His face had all melted together. His shoulders sagged. He just looked like a pile of disintegrating snow, and I didn't mind at all. I looked beyond him, toward the barn, and then I suddenly realized that something red was inching up the lane.

It was the snowplow.

And then everything sort of happened at once.

I let out a shout, the dogs barked, Mrs. MacMinnies said, "And about time, too!" and all the Littles came charging down the stairs looking as though their clothes had been blown on to them by a hurricane, and we all stood there in the window, cheering deliriously as the snowplow came toward us like some wonderful monster, heaving the snow to one side as it made its stately advance.

Then we saw that there was a truck behind it.

"It's that Charlie Murphy!" Mrs. MacMinnies announced.

"His name, Mrs. MacMinnies, is Charlie Murofino," Amanda told her.

Mrs. MacMinnies spread her gloved hands on her hips.

"I don't see why anyone would want to change their name to something fancy," she said severely. "Murphy's a good enough name for anyone. There's nothing to be ashamed of in being Irish!"

There was no arguing about it just then because, bumping along behind Charlie's old pickup truck was another truck with the telephone company's insignia painted on its side. And behind that was a station wagon. It was a regular parade.

"Holy mackerel!" Obie cried. "The whole United States Marine Corps is coming to our rescue!"

And then, as one man, we broke out into the "William Tell Overture."

We had to wait while the plow lurched forward and the other vehicles barreled along in the smooth track it made.

Before we knew it, the kitchen was full of people: Charlie, sad-eyed as ever, but grinning from ear to ear like the Saint Bernard dog that he really was this time, and the doctor, who had been in the station wagon, and the repairman from the telephone company, and the man from the snowplow, all stamping snow off their boots as they greeted us.

Then, suddenly, I caught a glimpse of someone else: someone familiar and unexpected and welcome. It was the Old Man.

He stood in the doorway, smiling at the lot of us in undisguised relief. I ran to him. He swung me around a few times, then he went and hugged everyone, including Mrs. MacMinnies, who couldn't decide whether to appear ruffled or pleased.

"I've been trying to get through to you on the telephone for days," the Old Man said.

"It was out of order, Jim," Aunt Claire told him.

"I know," he said. "When I finally heard from Mr. Murofino and got James's message, I thought it was pretty strange, so I grabbed the early train. I had to come up and see for myself what was going on. Mr. Murofino met me at the station. Now, are you all all right?"

Uncle Oliver looked surprised. He said that of course we were. We'd only had a little snow, that was all: or nearly all.

Charlie said, "I couldn't get the plow to come up last night. It was stuck on the road. But Ed Hill here was able to get it up your hill this morning."

Ed Hill smiled shyly and said he was sorry he couldn't make it any earlier, and anyway, it was a snap this morning because it was melting just enough.

Mrs. MacMinnies had already gotten another pot of coffee going on the stove.

Charlie said, "I brought your mail up from the box this time. I hope there wasn't anything important," and he handed a bundle of stuff to Uncle Oliver.

The doctor said, "Where's the patient?"

"Down at the barn, Doc," Charlie said. "The boys had better come with us. And you, too, Mr. Little."

I turned to the Old Man.

"Did you bring it?" I asked anxiously.

"Yes, James, I did," he said. He took it from his briefcase and handed it to me. "What I want to know, though," he added with a quizzical look, "is what in the world you wanted it for at a time like this."

"I'll tell you later," I said. I tucked it inside my shirt. I didn't want to look at it just then, with everybody milling around. It was too important, and if I'd been wrong I'd look like the worst kind of fool. I figured I'd waited that long to find out, I might as well wait a few more minutes.

We trudged down to the barn then: Charlie and the doctor and Obie and I. The Old Man said he might as well come along, so he walked beside me, his arm lightly thrown over my shoulder. Amanda was dying to come, too, but the doctor had said that maybe the ladies had better stay where they were.

Barney was there, all right. Nothing was changed: he lay spread-eagled on the straw, and while Charlie and the doctor and the Old Man went down through the trapdoor to look him over, I stole a quick glance at what the Old Man had brought.

Well, my hunch had been right, but it made me feel sort of dizzy to realize it. You don't usually expect a long shot like that to pay off. What the Old Man had brought with him was one of my collection of "Men Wanted" notices: the fourth one to the left in the second row over my bed. That was where I'd seen Barney's face before. And here it was, right enough, all down in black and white, with the words WANTED FOR ARMED ROBBERY over it. Only the name was different. And he had a beard in the picture, which was why no one around Jonesboro had spotted him in all the time he'd been there. But with the growth of stubble on his face his resemblance to the picture was unmistakable.

I showed it to Obie.

He read it carefully. Then he read it all over again, as though he were trying to memorize every word.

His eyes had a funny look of respect in them when they met mine. I won't deny that it was pretty gratifying. But all he said was "Wow!"

"That's why he wouldn't leave the place!" I said. "He was afraid he might get picked up. Why, he must have been hiding out on Walkaway Hill all the time, only he was alias Barney Rudkin!"

Obie nodded excitedly.

"And that's why he was looking for the money: he needed it to make his getaway."

We were staring at each other when the others came back up the ladder.

"That was a close thing," the doctor was saying. "The injection I gave him will pull him through, but it'll take time. And right now I've got to get him to a hospital. He'll be comfortable enough in my station wagon, if you'll give me a hand getting him in. I'll go and get the wagon now."

While we waited for him to return I showed the notice to Charlie and Uncle Oliver.

Uncle Oliver, for once, was speechless.

The Old Man gaped at me. He looked a little dazed. "Never in my wildest dreams," he murmured.

Charlie let out a long slow whistle.

"That explains a lot of things," he said. His grin seemed to light up the whole place. "You're quite a detective, James. Frankly, I thought you were off the beam, or just pulling some kid stuff, when you asked me to tell your father to send it up here special delivery." He scratched his chin. "Well, that sort of wraps things up, doesn't it? And you're the one who did it, all right."

I did my best to look modest. I mean, it was something I'd never imagined would happen to me. Here I was, sort of a hero, after all.

Fortunately, the doctor rolled up in the station wagon just then, and we were too busy getting Barney Rudkin into it to talk any further about all that. I noticed, however, that Charlie took the doctor aside and spoke to him, in an earnest way, so I guess the doctor was let in on it. I suppose even sick criminals have to be guarded. I couldn't help being a little sorry for Barney, though. He looked so gaunt and weak and helpless when we carried him out: not like a desperate criminal at all, but more like some poor wild animal that had been hunted down. Now that he had been captured, the Phantom of Walkaway Hill seemed a pitiful creature.

We watched the station wagon roll down the cleared lane. Then we made tracks back to the house. The telephone company's truck passed us on the way and the repairmen shouted out the window that the phone was working fine again.

As we came in the door Aunt Claire waved something at us. Her face was all glowing and the thing in her hand was a riot of color, like a handful of summer flowers.

"What in the world is that, Claire?" Uncle Oliver wanted to know.

"It came at last!" she cried. "It was with the rest of the mail."

"What came?" her asked, looking bewildered.

"The seed catalogue, for my garden!" Her gaze traveled out over the fields of melting snow. "It looks," she said happily, "as though spring will be here soon after all!"

The Old Man let himself down into a chair.

"I have never been so utterly confused in my life," he declared. His regard slowly moved from face to face. "All right," he said. "Start explaining. And don't leave anything out."

Well, we all settled down to have breakfast; that is, if you can call what we did settling down. Charlie joined us. And we proceeded to tell the Old Man the whole story, from beginning to end. It all poured out in a wild rush. Whenever one of us stopped talking, somebody else took up the thread. The Old Man sat there letting his coffee grow cold and looking as though he didn't believe a word of it.

Finally, Uncle Oliver produced the will, which made even Charlie Murofino goggle.

"And so," Uncle Oliver concluded, "while everything else we have is pure Sterling, Walkaway Hill is pure Maggie."

"I would like to see with my own eyes this astonishing shaggy canine," the Old Man said.

"Just look out the window," Amanda told him. "There she is."

And sure enough, there was Maggie, lying out in the middle of the snow, like a genial tawny lion, her mane fleecy, her eyes clear, peacefully guarding her home. Sieglinde lay nearby, trying to look equally noble and distinguished, and almost succeeding. When Maggie saw us at the window she pricked up her ears. Then she yawned prodigiously and tucked her nose under her flank.

The Old Man shook his head in wonder. Then he got up.

"Well, James," he said, "are you all ready? It's time to get going. Our train leaves within the hour."

It didn't take me long to pack. Obie helped. When we came down with my stuff, Aunt Claire turned to Mrs. MacMinnies.

"Well, Mrs. MacMinnies," she said. Her voice was sort of choky and distressed. "I guess it's time. I mean—I suppose you'll be leaving now."

Mrs. MacMinnies looked around the room.

Then, deliberately and without a word, she removed the hat with the purple feather and took off her coat. She put on her checked apron.

We watched her with amazement.

"I'm staying," she said. "I guess it's livelier here after

all than it would be with my married cousin in Brooklyn. And besides, the dear knows what you Littles would ever do without me." A smile broke like the sun across her wintry features. "Sure," said she, "if we live through the winter, the Devil wouldn't kill us in summer."

"Please God," amended Amanda.

"Please God!" said Mrs. MacMinnies.

Charlie was already outside. Now we heard his truck's motor starting up.

The Old Man took my valise.

He was smiling at me. He even seemed a little proud. I mean, it looked as though he was really glad to have me back with him for a while. I suddenly realized that the Old Man had missed me.

"Ready, son?" he said.

"Sure," I said. "I'm ready."

After all, the adventure was over. The rest was all to come out later: the will turned out to be valid, after all. Amanda's conjectures as to why Barney behaved the way he did turned out to be correct. As for the reward for the discovery and capture of Alias Barney Rudkin, that turned out to be a disappointment. Obie and I didn't get a chance to touch a dollar of it. It was put away "in trust" for our future education. Future education indeed!

So I didn't really mind going. I knew that Easter vacation would be around in less than a month, and it would be fun to help Aunt Claire with the garden and see what Walkaway Hill was like in spring.

And then I suddenly realized that the adventure of Walkaway Hill wasn't entirely finished. There was still all that money of Mrs. Houghton's to look for.

I winked at Obie and Amanda.

They winked solemnly back. They knew what I meant. Even DeeDee knew, this time.

Outside, Charlie was leaning on his horn.

I looked up at the Old Man.

"Home, James!" the Old Man said.

CELEBRATING

YEARLING

25 YEARS

Yearling Books
celebrates its
25 years—
and salutes
Reading Is
Fundamental®
on its 25th
anniversary.